An EMP Tale of Two Towns

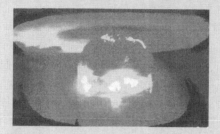

Contrasting stories of life in two towns exposed to the same Electromagnetic Pulse burst - One was protected; the other was not.

- Even protected town had some problems
- Amazing & uncivilized lessons learned
- Many EMP protection options discovered
- What the future predicts

There is always a good side to any disaster

- New Products & Services created
- New Markets opened
- Millions of new jobs developed

by Donald R.J. White, PE
EMP Solutions, and
Renewable Energy Creations, LLC

18 July 2013, 02:30

Book Summary

This "non-fiction novel" helps prevent the destruction of electricity and electronics that instantly results from an upper atmospheric detonation of a nuclear weapon (HEMP = High altitude Electromagnetic Pulse) by a terrorist or rogue nation. Over roughly a 500-1,000 mile ground radius, a HEMP explosion burns out most computers, electronic-control systems, telecommunication and transportation devices. Airplanes lose control; vehicles dysfunction; elevators get stuck; subways stop; lighted structures go dark; radio and TV cease; and commerce comes to a near halt. Humans are not killed: infrastructure remains physically intact. Scientists, military, industry and others testifying before Congress say this is an event waiting to happen - "Not if, but when. (Ed. note: acronym "EMP" is used hereafter instead of "HEMP" since Internet avoids confusion with keyword "hemp", a special cloth, rope and marijuana.)

The USA Dept. of Defense has EMP protected it's Navy ships, other military structures, and selected government office buildings. Yet, little on EMP protection exists in the civil sector of commercial and residential infrastructures, solar farms and the electric grid. Therefore, these voids of protection provide new options in this *faction (factual fiction)* for EMP protecting new component and system hardware design with cost estimates, insurance, who pays and how.

This *"non-fiction novel"* is written mostly in the third person. It also provides a sequel to Forstchen's, *New York Times* bestseller, "One Second After" wherein he describes a catastrophic dysfunctional life following an EMP incident. My book describes two contrasting towns 200 miles apart in Virginia, both exposed to same EMP incident. The first town is not EMP protected. The other town is over 95% EMP protected. What an outstandingly enormous survival difference!

These two post-EMP town episodes are contrasted in each chapter, depicted in time sequence, such as the day of the EMP event, one week later, one month , etc. Each time elapse chapter also has a third part which is "lessons learned" from the post EMP events of the contrasting towns.. This goes on till one year later, in the final chapter, an enormous contrast is presented between the two towns via a remarkable but compassionate summary of lessons learned.

The novel part is a thriller and written for the general public level in order that the lay can follow the action. It is also highly illustrated by drawings, graphs, diagrams, charts, tables, and photos to support the text and tutorials.

Shielded solar rooftops are a major part of an EMP protection plan and survival, since, with few exceptions, batteries and generator and fuel shortage cannot handle the electrical load when electric grid goes down. Plan for this while producing new products and services, opening new markets, and prospering from income and jobs so generated. That's what this "non-fiction" novel combo offers all readers.

Enjoy the thriller as you read; follow the material and apply its teachings.

Disclaimer

This is a non-fiction novel (faction) written mostly in the third person. It is based on the wide consensus of many informed articles, books and authors of today re what the presence is and what the future of EMP may portend. But, this especially contains our own additions as well. There is no guarantee or assertion that any or all will happen.

The author, a retired engineer and CEO, has applied his 50 years of exposure in the Electromagnetic Compatibility field to do his best portrayal of what is perceived to be coming and what some of the consequences may be. Thus, there is no disclaimer as there is no guarantee either.

Read this and hope that an EMP event as described herein never happens. There is one bright side to the "non-fiction" novel and that is the development of new products and services and generating marketing outlets that produce millions of new jobs.

Read; become sober; Wake up America & enjoy. But act now.

Printed in the United States of America
Library of Congress PCN: (in process)
Library of Congress Cataloging-in-Publication Date:
Library of Congress Card Number: (in process)
ISBN 978-1490427911
Sku: 1477478450

Acknowledgments

This non-fiction novel, *"Contrast Survival Lifestyles – A Tale of Two Towns"* is based on a mixture of some international threats, scientific and engineering principles, and some forecasts. This *faction is* dedicated to the Glory of God – the Epitome of Truth – and a prayer that the content will never happen.

The author expresses thanks to those who reviewed this faction including his wife, Colleen, Wayne and Joan Pilikian, Dona Loope and Royce White.

I will contribute 10% of all sales of this book to charity including *Grace Presbyterian Church* of Lake Suzy, FL 34269, USA, the *Wounded Warrior* Project seen on TV, and SonLight Power, a small solar installation company who, for free, brings both solar electricity and the Bible to schools, clinics and churches in impoverished locations in Central America and Africa.

Enjoy.

That some achieve great success, is proof to all that others can achieve it as well."
Abe Lincoln

Contents

Scenario Assumptions in this Book

About nuclear EMP protection, America is in disbelief and apathetic about its view regarding "be prepared" - the boy scout motto. US is distracted with a weak economy, high unemployment and deep debt. The effectiveness of a single high-altitude electromagnetic pulse (EMP) over a major geographical region is far more painfully and devastatingly protracting then both the Hiroshima and Nagasaki, atomic bombs of WWII. Scientists, military flag officers and congressmen have testified and say EMP is an event waiting to happen, viz., "Not if – but when?"

USA has spent billions in EMP hardening (protecting) its naval fleet, weapons and ammo storage and selected intelligence and other office buildings. In contrast the civil sector of residential, commercial, industrial infrastructure and utilities, are totally unprepared. There does not even exist a wide awareness or directory of expectations, understandings and options for actions to be taken or to be ready for that eventful day. An EMP event would make 9-11 and Pearl Harbor look like cakewalks.

Thus, this book is written as a novel because (1) it is a scary and sobering thriller to read, while (2) it develops a wide EMP understanding, corrective actions, and motivations toward becoming prepared. But How? The assumptions are that the most difficult part of getting started, is getting started. It is of questionable value for isolated or scattered homes and commercial buildings to become EMP protected, since after an EMP burst, the power grid will go down and nearly all electronics will become dysfunctional. Then food, water, medication and fuel replenishment are lost as well. The bottom line is that people slowly die of food starvation and poisoning, disease epidemics, no medication or fuel, and many or most vehicles will be inoperable.

Conclusion: A nuclear EMP surviving entity must be made up from many elements living together to provide the product and services necessary to mutually sustain life. Considering the lack of consumption - good replenishment stores, supporting vehicles, and regional distribution centers, the smallest entity of any significant chance for survival lifestyle, may be a complete village defined herein as a collection of roughly 1,000 inhabitants. The next better entity is a town of 10,000 people. Then, a city of 100,000 or more inhabitants. Too small an entity cannot survive with any pretext of lifestyle due to lack of the basic survival replenishments. Too large an entity, such as a big city, becomes difficult to activate, enforce and finance at least in early stages. So, this book compromises and selects the level of a town of 10,000 inhabitants for best performance. This includes a roughly 10-mile agriculture ring around the town where multiple crops and animals are grown for food production.

The size must be chosen carefully to be representative of USA since it will become a database and template for future reference, in whole or in part, multiplied a thousand times throughout USA when implemented. It should not be limited to an East or West Coast, near-ocean town since boat or ship access cannot be enjoyed by extrapolation to 90% of the remaining population. Conversely, it should not be in the middle of the nation, since a large body of water should be available within, say, several hundred miles to increase replenishments from ships originating outside USA and reshipped by rail or air..

The next decision: Should a selected EMP protected town become "a best-held secret" so that curiosity and database seeking visitors are not constantly bombarding the town?

Also, in the event of the first EMP burst, the town might even be invaded by neighbors with huge battles ensuing because of their survival resources and wherewithal. On the other hand, maybe the town should have a large museum to house all manor of educational EMP-preparedness exhibits, movies and videos. Daily bus tours would take the visitors around town on a two-hour ride showing them residential and commercial EMP-protected installations with protected solar rooftops, etc. In short, the town becomes a nuclear EMP protection showcase for the benefit of the rest of the nation and it's planners and implementers.

The final decision involves who pays for this EMP protection and how? Since the entire nation and all states stand to gain from valuable information origination from a few pilot towns, most of the cost should be funded by elements outside of those towns. This can be done by issuing county bonds and selling insurance with monthly or periodic premiums. To this is added a modest Fed and State pay-in as they participate in developing more national EMP protection templates. Then, each protected property owner pays only a low cost, monthly insurance premium based on payments heretofore paid the electric utility for it's electricity. Also, the EMP protection museum income and bus tours add to the revenue sources and fiscal viability of the pilot towns.

So the name of this book is *"Contrasting EMP Survivals– A Tale of Two Towns"* = an exciting novel filled with surprises and contrasts, having an ending that each reader must judge for himself.

"Ask not what America will do for you, but what together we can do for the freedom of man." JFK

Prologue: About the Book Format and Structure

Bestville, a town in Central Virginia, has been selected as the recipient of a nearly complete nuclear EMP (electromagnetic pulse) protection. This, and a few others, are orchestrated by the state and federal government, to gain an enormous pragmatic database for the future possible replication in whole or in part throughout USA. While it is hoped that an EMP event will never happen, we must plan to end our lethargy by becoming aware and being prepared. (visit: www.emp-safeguard. com for more EMP details)

The book story pattern is that each chapter progresses in time from the nuclear event first day till one year later, contrasting the aftermath in two Virginia towns, 200 miles apart. Cantdo is representative of most other villages, town or city in the USA with essentially no civil EMP protection. (Not even an awareness program of education while the Internet is replete with stories, and many myths). Thus, each chapter has three parts: (1) short story about the unprotected town happenings and conversational or observation comments, (2) simultaneous EMP event with its impact, remarks and comments in another town – this one EMP protected, and (3) observations, lessons learned, recommendations and correction details for avoiding the horrifying aftermath eventually

Nuclear EMP Survival Book Chapter Contents

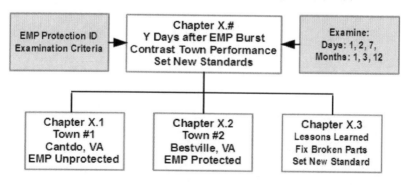

turning into madness and crime. Should readers still desire further rationale and technical details, they may be found in the author's companion unclassified EMP-safeguard book containing 105 drawings, sketches, diagrams, spreadsheets, tables, charts, graphs, and photos, available from website: www.emp-safeguard.com or at Amazon and elsewhere. Title: *EMP – Protect Family, Homes and Community* (see page 154 for some details)

Options for Reading this Book.

This book can be read in one of three ways, depending upon the preference and missions of each reader. For example:

1.- *A scary and suspense thriller story*. Read part 1.X only of each chapter, e.g: 1.1, 2.1, 3.1, etc for life in Cantdo, Va the unprotected USA town following an EMP burst. In other words, skip all X.2 and X.3, as they will distract your focus.

Default: Read sequence 1.1, 2.1, 3.1, etc. as just mentioned, as this is the thriller of what happened at Cantdo with no EMP protection. Then, read 1.2, 2.2, 3.2.... next to see what EMP protection at Bestville really does. Thus, go now to page 917 and start your read.

2.- *An analyst wanting to simultaneously contrast the Tale of Two Towns*. Still exciting, but want a better view of the benefits (and some discovered weaknesses) of the EMP-protected town, Bestville, over the the unprotected town, Cantdo. Thus, Read 1.1, and 1,2; then 2.1 and 2.2, ... X.1 and X.2. Skip all X.3 parts.

3.- *Industry, independent professional and government planners*. All third parts of each chapter, X.3, is your focus because it portrays lessons learned, options for fixes, and what the future predicts. Of course, you will also need to read the X.1 and X.2 parts first in order to know the problems needing to be fixed, some of which are quite subtle. But, X.3 is where you will see the helpful information conveyed and the challenges.

Individuals who Play a Role in this Faction

About 25 widely different individuals play an important role in this faction (faction = "hybrid" word for "fiction" or novel based on facts, where possible). Refer to this page as necessary in case you forget who they are.

List of Characters and Places Sited in the Non-Fiction Novel									
			Chapter			Chapter			
Name	Who?	Where?	1	2	3	4	5	6	7
Hank Drinkwell	Brothers	Cantdo	X		X				X
Jerry Drinkwell	Bothers	Cantdo	X		X				X
Jennie Drinkwell	Sister	Cantdo				X			
Tom Drinkwell	Dad	Cantdo				X			
Don Follow	Uncle/Hospital	Cantdo				X			X
Hopkins	Asst Principal	Cantdo	X						
Ken Atwater	1980 Pontiac	Cantdo	X				X		
Pete Henderson	Town Mayer	Bestville		X			X		
Mark Swanson	Town Mayer	Cantdo				X			
Chris Blue	Power Engineer	Cantdo				X			
Ted Barron	Substation Engr	Bestville					X		
Harold Schultz	Chief of Police	Bestville					X	X	
Anderson Family	Survivalists	Cantdo							X
Zack Thompson	Local Coll Prof	Bestville			X				
Mike Tolstoy	Chief of Police	Cantdo				X	X		
Bill Matovich	Fish & Wildlife	Cantdo				X			
Tony Costello	Town Supervisor	Bestville				X		X	
Harold Johnson	Town Banker	Bestville				X			
Andy Moreland	Hospital	Bestvile				X			
Dr. Blemming		Cantdo					X		
Governor Maxwell	VA Governor	Virginia					X		
Dr. Smallwood	Dentist	Cantdo					X		
John Garwood	Director, EDO	Bestville					X		
Organization	Who?	Where?	1	2	3	4	5	6	7
Audioband Hearing	Hearing Aid	Bestville	X						
Food & Drug Admin	MS-461, RS-105	Bestville	X						
Barr EMC Corp	EMP Contractors	Bestville	X						
Well-Mart	Huge Super Store	Cantdo		X		X			
Stoberton	Town 60 miles	Bestville		X			X		
Timothy Shell Station	Gas Station	Cantdo			X				
Ames Funeral Home	Undertaker	Cantdo				X			
Jeston	local Coll Proff	Bestville				X			
Spikes Gun Shopp	Gun Store	Cantdo					X		
Chesapeake Naval Base	Norfolk, VA	Cantdo					X		
Organization	Who?	Where?	1	2	3	4	5	6	7

Chapter 1

Cantdo & Bestville, VA, Burst Day

1.1 Cantdo, VA, Spring, at 3:00 p.m. (Unprotected Town. Day of the EMP Burst)

Harris High School was letting out at 3:00 p.m. when students exiting the building noticed strangely that some cars and school buses were frozen-like in their different street positions. A few vehicle owners were seen gathered around their opened car hoods trying to determine what had just happened and the cause. One was seen running down the street seeking help.

A student ran back into the building to alert others of a strange street situation. Others outside started to call home on their cell phones and ipads. But, all mobile phone units were seen to be dysfunctional. Nothing appeared to work, whereupon frustration and confusion set in.

Meanwhile, the student who ran back into the building noticed others gathered around the assistant principal's office. One was trying to resuscitate him as he appeared to have expired – no breathing, or pulse. At that moment the principal reappeared to announce that Mr. Hopkins had a heart pacemaker which may have gone bad. But how? The secretary said she tried to call 9-11, but the phone had no dial tone.

More confusion and disbelief set in on the gathering group.

Additional students exiting the building were quickly informed by the early birds of the weird disarray of vehicles and dysfunctional cell phones and ipads. While those having bikes quickly departed for home, others began to speculate at the curb about just what is happening. Then, one student said this looks like a scene from a book his dad was reading, called "One Second After". He said his dad remarked that a high altitude nuclear weapon burst would wipe out the electric grid and burn out nearly all electronics for hundreds of miles, maybe up to a thousand, while humans would not feel a thing on the ground. "Oh, my God", replied another. "Is this happening to us?" He added, "Maybe more are to follow and the next may be more destructive." Then, the group discussion became somewhat hysterical as more disbelief, fear and anxiety developed.

Most students had to walk home and noticed similar dysfunctional vehicles on the way. Many homeowners were seen in front of their homes and out in the street talking about the perplexing situation. Later upon arriving home, the two Harris High brothers, Hank and Jerry Drinkwell, also confirmed that the electricity was out and houses were dark. Also, their mother reported that the radio and TV were dead as well, and the house phones were not working.

Neighbors gathered in small groups speculating on what happened and what to do next. One observed that his old 1980 Pontiac hardtop was still working. Another said he had no water after flushing the toilet more than once. A third remarked that he had about 11,000 gallons of water in his home pool. He asked for opinions on how his water may become drinkable. The group speculated about the incongruity of events: No obvious terrorist attack as people, infrastructure and buildings are not destroyed. Yet, the electricity is gone.

But, why no functional cells, radio and TV especially since some devices are battery operated?

Ken Atwater, a Pontiac car owner, returned to the group discussion. He had turned on his car radio and all he could get was static across the AM and FM bands. There were no stations from other Virginia cities or elsewhere? So one remarked, "What do we do now? We can't call the power company or emergency services; there appears to be no functional phones or vehicles?"

Jerry Drinkwell replied, "Oh my gosh! The frozen food in the fridge will go bad and we may run out of food, water and medication for grandma." Hank, Jerry's brother, remarked, "Help! Let's bike now over to Cantdo Shopping Mall and investigate. While it is nearing dusk, we have lights on our bikes, but maybe they won't work; there's almost no traffic, and maybe we can pick up some canned goods in the food center while there".

1.2, Bestville, VA, at 3:00 p.m. (EMP Protected Town)

Because of sudden EMP electric power outage warnings from transfer alarms and sirens used at 3:02 p.m., Bestville, the EMP protected town, folks were informed that unless already in use, their backup power is activated. Unknown to most, whether at home, work, shopping mall, or elsewhere, their solar rooftop and back-up batteries are operational (already) or taken over from the electric utility power loss.

Nearly all car and truck vehicles were operational, and most cell phones, ipads and laptops and e-book readers were working, but only for local communication within their Bestville township. Distant located source radio and TV broadcast, telephone and cell service were non functional. Satellite communications to distant non-EMP event locations and fiber-optic links continued to work. The one local radio station was functional with news of the emergency announcements. The principal reasons being that their buildings are all EMP protected and each has its own protected solar rooftop, battery bank and generator.

Later, it was surprisingly discovered that nearly all electrical and electronics were dysfunctional in one food market. This means no cash register or air conditioning was working. Also, there was no lights, no public address, etc. Explanations for this apparent anomaly, were that the store failed to construct a double door and vestibule entry to prevent EMP leakage if

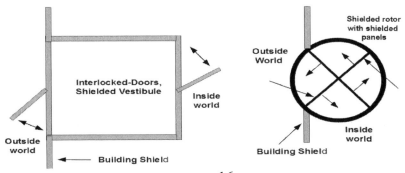

the event happened at the very moment of a person entering or exiting the building as shown in the illustration.

Following redundant confirmation at 3:12 p.m. of the EMP event: (1) the town sirens gave alert notice as did (2) the launching of several loud-speaker vehicles traveling the streets of Bestville. further, the above announced radio station reminded all listeners that the inevitable EMP event, regrettably, has just happened. This means the following actions and recommendations apply as stated in the prologue of your EMP warning and preparation books. A surprisingly well controlled response by the listeners, demonstrated the value of the many weeks and months of indoctrination and training. In other words, Bestville, so far, seemed to have practiced the Boy-Scouts' motto, "Be prepared." But wait! We have only just started....

One elevator was stuck in the hospital between floors. A later maintenance check showed that the electronic elevator controls, are located inside of a shack on the roof. Apparently, the bonding of the shack to the rooftop screen was not properly done by the installer. Of more concern, inside that shack on the EMP test confirmation clipboard form, the installation EMP shielding test was either never done or not recorded, a clear lack of quality control. Perhaps, this was a victim of the lack of wide experience in building shielding.

By the way, Audiobond Hearing Co., received a few phone calls that their clients, who were outdoors when the EMP event took place, reported that their hearing aids stopped working. Later it was determined that nearly all medical devices have never been tested to meet EMP exposure levels, other than another maximum spec at 100 V/m of RS-105. What does the FDA have to say about this?

On the positive side, the town Mayer, Pete Henderson, his

staff and Barr EMC Corporation received a lot of credit for the remarkable EMP protection that their company and others have done to make Bestville relatively EMP immune.

1.3 Cantdo-Bestville, Lessons Learned, Burst Day

Outside of an EMP protected building, all electronic devices such as cells and ipads carried by individuals at the moment of an EMP burst, would be burned out. However, in anticipation, the town plan called for residents to have a backup cell phone, inside of a shielded aluminum foil envelope to be carried only when traveling outside of an EMP protected home or commercial or industrial building.

The big difference at Bestville is that the entire town has been thoroughly educated and trained about Nuclear EMP, the threats it presents, options for survival solutions, and the supporting participation subsidy that every property owner has received as a national experiment. They are one of several towns in USA who has undergone this civil EMP protection and citizens are very grateful. Additionally, each pays a relatively small monthly insurance premium for the pro-tection beyond their solar rooftop replacing their earlier electric utility bills.

They all agreed to keep this survival experiment (Town EMP Survival Protection Plan, #1 in the org chart diagram below) a relative "secret" or low-key to the outside world so there would be little to no press and other media. One potential concern is that if the neighboring towns are fully informed of Bestville, it may be invaded by curiosity seekers, and especially inundated by outsiders seeking refuge when a real nuclear event appears. However the latter is greatly curtailed by the dysfunctional non-EMP-protected vehicles and others fully preoccupied with their own post-EMP problems. If later it is really deemed to be a significant problem, this could possibly be avoided if Bestville were located inside of a military Air Force base or other such protected area.

Returning to the protection plan org chart, in charge of this special situation is the chairman of a consortium consisting of representative(s) of the local county *Economic Development Office*, the Chamber of Commerce, a few of the larger local manufacturing, construction and real estate companies (see box #2) plus a few private professionals: architects, engineers, lawyers and accountants.

The diagram also shows (box #3) some of the funding sources which are primarily insurance companies, local bonds sold by the county, local banks and some R&D and related funding from the State and Federal government. While it may not be believed necessary, a few sponsors may also be invited.

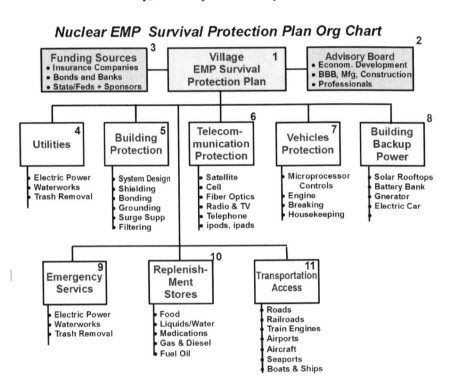

Nuclear EMP Survival Protection Plan Org Chart

The second row (Boxes #4-8) in the org chart shows the sectors necessary to make the whole EMP-protection plan work. It is the backbone of the "how-to-do-it" options discussed elsewhere in this book. They include utilities (#4); building EMP protection products and supporting services (the EMC or Electromagnetic Compatibility companies); telecommunications infrastructure, both local and contact with outside of Bestville where some other transceivers, satellite relay or other networks may be working. Block 2 in the chart also shows vehicle protection via update retrofit kits to shield and filter microprocessor (digital control circuits) and some shielded wiring. Box #8 represents the protected screened solar rooftop together with batteries and generator for 24/7 electric power in a situation having a dead electric grid.

Only the electric utility in box #4 is indefinitely replaced by the solar rooftop, batteries and generators in box #8. Since the water pumps and/or their controls are burned out during an EMP incident, their electrical/electronic parts must be EMP protected to ensure water distribution to all consumers. A large community water tank, would only provide water for perhaps a week. If the source is a reservoir or stream at an elevation above the village, an endless supply may be available. These are not the answers.

The third row in the org chart shows the priority for EMP protection: (box #9) emergency services of police, fire, and accident response units. The replenishment stores (box #10) are very important as they provide food and liquids for basic survival, medication from pharmacies and fuel (gasoline and diesel) for vehicles, without which we would die within a week, or so.

The subject of supplies from distant distribution centers to refurbish the shelves of the local stores becomes a very compelling discussion later on since their availability in both supply content and transportation ability become paramount.

21

Finally in the the org chart, box #11 speaks to the broader subject of transportation. How far out does or should Bestville have to reach in providing *replenishing* groceries, water, medications and fuel for both vehicles and heating a home or building? Perhaps, one answer may be for each town of 10,000± population to have its own small airfield (runway not less than 4,000 ft.) capable of take off and landing small-medium cargo planes (even a Globemaster III) and/or a single railroad siding where EMP hardened or old steam engines can bring in train loads of replenishments. These issues and options are answered in subsequent chapters as *The Tale of Two Towns* unfolds.

Note: Far greater details on EMP hardening are provided by the author's other EMP Protection Book, *"EMP – Protect Family, Homes and Community."*

Chapter 2

One Day Later

2.1 Cantdo, VA (EMP Unprotected Town), Day 1

Word spread from mouth to mouth that the mayor, Mark Swanson, was to speak at 10:00 a.m. at the town plaza gazebo on the first day after the disaster event. Many of the population walked or arrived by bicycle and realized by then that there were no working computers, no Skype no teleconferencing; no radio; no TV nor any other way of communicating since it was quickly understood by most people that all electronics were indeed not functioning in addition to no electric utility power and no running water.

At 10:05 the meeting began, Mayor Swanson announced for all to come up close to the podium, bringing your bicycles as he had no public address system nor any other way to speak except at nearly a shouting level. He said his battery megaphone and backup generator were not working. His remarks then turned to a prayer to God to bless Cantdo and our entire nation as the mayor yet had no idea as to the expanse of their disaster exposure. He then introduced three people who would speak: the local hospital co-diretor, the chief of police, and a utility engineer who would first explain what is believed to have happened.

The electric power engineer, Chris Blue, said he is in charge of the 5th and Monroe street substation from which most of the town gets its electric power from the power plant. It then distributes the power around Cantdo via their overhead and buried local power lines.

He said, "To those of you who understand the phenomena, we have had an EMP, or nuclear Electromagnetic Pulse explosion – not a Solar Flare, such as a Geomagnetic Storm. The latter would represent at most a possible loss of the electric grid power. However, since the loss also contains no working radio, TV, phones and the like, only an upper atmosphere EMP explosion can do that since humans also do not feel a thing (Ed. caveat: those with heart pacemakers and hearing aids may have their devices burned out) and all infrastructure remains in tact. We are trying to learn what all this means and portends as we have not paid much attention to some of the earlier EMP warnings. I will report more tomorrow after I do more discovery."

"Meanwhile, we are not able to communicate with other villages, towns, or cities since we have lost all telecommunications. One car radio was found to pick up some long distance AM broadcast last night from locations believed to be over about 500 miles away."

Engineer Blue continued, "With few exceptions, we cannot drive anywhere or expect to receive out-of-town visitors since their vehicles are probably less than 20 years old and inclined to be more EMP susceptible due to their micro-processors. Our one long railroad siding and small 4,000 ft. air strip have had no traffic to inform us of what is going on outside of Cantdo. With that, I will turn you back over to Mayor Swanson."

Meanwhile, revisit the home of the Harris High School brothers, Hank and Jerry Drinkwell, at 10:00 a.m. Since school is closed, they just returned from a second store visit by bicycle; this one to Well-Mart. The huge store was partly opened, but no lights except skylights and some fueled lanterns as the generators and microprocessor controls were all presumed to be burned out. Also, The refrigerated foods and beverage cases were still a little cool and people were taking out remaining contents, because there were posted, hand-written signs inviting them to do so, for free.

However, over in the canned goods section things were very different and somewhat ugly. The shelves were nearly empty and a few simultaneous arguments could be seen as people fought over who arrived there first. In one aisle, where there was only French bread and a few dozen other loaves left, a nasty fist fight erupted there. A few citizens tried to break up the battle and cool down emotions.

Cash registers were not working. Customers had to pay cash (no credit cards) and all items purchased had to be added up by hand by the cashier. Lines were very slow moving with very long waits. Shoe boxes were used as money containers.

The Well-Mart pharmaceutical section was in total disarray as some people had already ransacked the inside presumably in search of specific medications. It develops that the store manager had made the difficult decision to open the store to the food center and pharmaceuticals only with all other sections cordoned off. With no police or vehicles moving, and the canned goods shelves empty, the manager later decided to secure the entire building from further entry using only a handful of available employees.

Hank and Jerry's uncle, Don Follow, an assistant physician, arrived at their house after the Well-Mart trip to announce Cantdo's only hospital has about four days supply of fuel to run two surviving old non-electronic controlled generators; the others were already dysfunctional. Thus, hospital hallways and most room lights are dimmed or out. Air conditioning was not working at all as their electronic controllers were also dysfunctional. Besides, they did not have enough generator fuel or power capacity to run them 24/7 anyway. Some COPD patients who require oxygen could no longer have this as the oxygen machine controllers are dead. While placed on tank oxygen, this would last for only two days at most. Refrigerated medications were only good for a few days as well. What then to do with all the hospital patients and employees, and lack of operational machines and devices?

The Drinkwell brothers and Uncle Don, also reported that two Cantdo citizens have died from unknown causes. The local undertaker could not get involved as his entire facility was without electricity and electronics. Funeral and burial services were unavailable for similar reasons. Also, no functional vehicles like a hearse for transport or backhoe for trench digging were available. In fact, the entire town of Cantdo, that offers services of all types, was shut down.

2.2 Bestville, VA (EMP Protected Town), Day 1

Many of the Bestville residents were tuned in on their one local radio station to learn the extent of what has happened in their own town and other locations within USA . They were able to do this as their radios were functional because their buildings were EMP protected and the Radio station was protected as well. Someone remarked that their external antennas had protective band-pass filters inserted to receive the broadcast inside of their shielded buildings, but otherwise had blocked the EMP from entry.

Mayor Henderson was making a number of announcements at 9:30 a.m.   Others in his group would speak about what was happening. After a brief introduction, the electric utility substation engineer; Ted Barron, reported that their satellite communication relay system, that connects to Richmond, the state capital and Washington, DC (special EMP protected also), disclosed the following.

We have had a presumed terrorist attack by an unidentified source(s) that launched three simultaneous EMP weapons over USA. For the West Coast and Central USA, enemy missiles were intercepted and destroyed by our military anti-missile missiles. However, the terrorist missile from a container ship detonated on the East Coast got through and exploded taking down electric power and destroying most electronics from South Carolina to Massachusetts on the North (800 miles), and from the Atlantic Ocean to Easten Ohio on the West (600 miles). Except for a few other EMP protected towns and some military base locations, Naval Ships, Intelligence buildings and selected other infrastructure, Bestville is the only central East Coast protected town. This radio station will keep you informed throughout the day with all updates.

The mayor then introduced the Chief of Police, Harold Shultz, and the director of the county Economic Development Office. Schultz said all listeners should review pages 11 through 14 of their EMP Emergency Planning Guide to refresh what to do and not to do regarding contacting family and friends and others in the EMP impacted areas. Remember, you can't communicate since their phones, cells, ipads and other communication units are almost certainly burned out. However, some satellite communications links may still be open.

Do not attempt to drive to any locations affected because (1) you will not be able to get gas or diesel fuel along the way, or especially (2) you may be stopped and your vehicle may be high jacked by desperate people. Also, the area may be under Marshall law and the national guard may stop you and force you to return to Bestville. Focus your energies on self survival of our Bestville town, at least for the present.

Mayor Henderson reminded all listeners and other Bestville residents that they were given a daily diary book to write down their experiences. These include, those relative to what equipment and the working condition of the electronics they own, dates and time. The option to do this using their computers is a practical alternative. These data will later be of great value to other county economic development offices, state governments and the Feds when they update their master EMP protection analysis and planning directory.

Meanwhile, back at the local Well-Mart, the town radio reporter and his photographer were documenting the activities. Some of the overhead electric lights were turned off as well as most of the A/C in the non-food center and pharmaceuticals areas to conserve generator fuel, although their solar rooftop can handle most of the electrical load during non overcast daytime.

Canned food goods were fairly picked over since there is no food distribution center in Bestville. The closest is Stoberton, 60 miles away and they are not known to survive the unprotected areas. However it was rumored that some replacement supplies may be arriving in about five days by our own wood-burning steam engine freight train and lesser quantities by air at our small local airfield. However, the uncertainties always causes people to hoard supplies for fear of the unknown in spite of all the indoctrination and preparation earlier on.

In summary, Mayer Henderson said, "Thank God and all those involved in the preparation work that went into making Bestville an EMP protected town. It is especially gratifying that very few folks lost their jobs such as those who receive and give directions to those outside of our township. However, remember, that for most of those receiving retirement and social service checks, this may be indefinitely discontinued. Thus our Plan, Zebra, discussed in the next chapter, goes into effect immediately for them.

2.3 Cantdo-Bestville, Lessons Learned, Day 1

Since the electricity blackout is now known to be from an EMP burst, not from a solar flare, the power grid loss may be due to burnout of substation system program logic controllers or SCADA (Supervisory Control and Data Acquisition) systems. It is presumed that they can be replaced in weeks. However many cascading units may be involved, including several power generating plants and or substations in the power outage area. Thus, the replacement time might run into months or longer. Meanwhile, however, the protected solar rooftop backup power in all EMP-protected Bestville buildings has taken over, moments after the EMP incident.

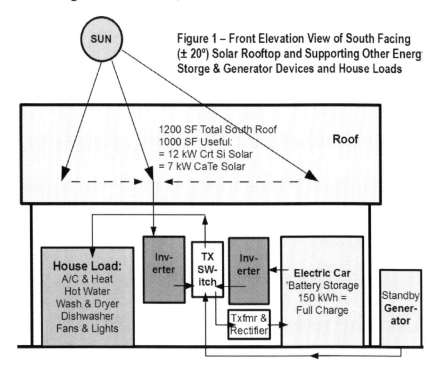

Figure 1 – Front Elevation View of South Facing (± 20°) Solar Rooftop and Supporting Other Energy Storge & Generator Devices and House Loads

(Note: Not shown in the drawing is the transfer switch between the electric power grid and the solar rooftop power. This can range from manual to automatic). The most important point that approved EMP surge suppressors are used on the power grid side to avoid burnout of the house or building electrical and electronics. Do not use lightning surge suppressors as they are roughly 100 times to slow and will not work.

Backup power consists of three general parts: (1) EMP protected Solar rooftop power panels and inverters, (2) battery banks, and (3) diesel-engine driven generator. This applies to a typical 2,000 sq. ft. home up to commercial buildings and industrial warehouses. The drawing above shows the general layout of a home and its major energy components. On bright sunshiny days, the median solar roof output provides typically about 8 kW (kilowatts) of power.

The solar developed energy goes (1) first to service the active household electric load with (2) excess energy being used to charge the independent battery bank or the electric vehicle's batteries, if applicable. The batteries stored energy (appx. 50 kWh) provide the electricity for overcast days and for lower-load nocturnal needs. Should the electric vehicle (acting as a battery bank) become discharged, the standby generator comes to the rescue. It is typically a 10-15 kW propane or diesel engine-driven generator. Depending on the storage tanks, there may be enough fuel for weeks or months, since the sun will always provide most of the daily needs.

The rest of the drawing shows the inverters which convert the low DC voltage output from the solar panels or from the electric vehicles to household 120/240V AC voltage. These run all the appliances and other electric loads. The transformer and rectifiers generate the correct DC voltage for charging the

31

battery bank or electric vehicle's batteries. The transfer switch connects the selected source for driving the household loads from the three energy sources.

If enough space in the garage exists, the generator can be located therein to avoid the need to EMP protect it as the entire house including garage is EMP protected as described later. In that event the generator fumes are exhausted to the outside via a waveguide-beyond-cutoff port in the exhaust line.

Typical median electric loads for the average home are roughly (varies significantly within the USA and location latitude):

Air Conditioning & electric heater = 2500 Watts
Refrigerator = 850 Watts
Hot Water heater = 1,000 W
Dishwasher = 800 Watts
Washer & dryer = 1500 Watts
Five fans = 450 Watts
Fluorescent light bulbs: 300 Watts
Computer & peripherals: 125 Watts
Other (miscellaneous): 1200 Watts
                              Total: 8,725 Watts

From this list a peak load (remember not all appliances are in use simultaneously) of roughly 7kW exists with a daily average load at the equinoxes (Mar 21 and Sept 21) of about 5 kW. There is still enough extra electricity to slowly charge the electric vehicle should one be used. The electric vehicle manufacturers may not permit this (void the warantee) because of the additional ageing placed on the battery system

For more information and details, the reader may want to read the companion book, *"Nuclear EMP Threats – Protect Family, Home and Community"*. This is available from Amazon or visit web site www.emp-safeguard.com.

Chapter 3

Two Days Later

3.1 Cantdo, VA (EMP Unprotected Town), Day 2

The few older running cars drained empty the underground gasoline tanks of Timothy, the nearby Shell station as it was the only known station in Cantdo without a disabled pump. Timothy had kept it as a landmark antique with active pump to remind many of the locals of yesteryear's nostalgia. All other Cantdo gas stations were presumed dysfunctional including others at Timothy's as well. However, later some used hand pumps.

More than 90% of the Cantdo employees were not at work as their buildings had no power and all electronic controls were known or presumed to be burned out. This included lights, the telephone systems, computers, printers, building temperature controllers, elevators, security alarms, water heaters, toilets, and so on. Thus, folks are at home helping to focus more on family and friends survival.

Hank, Jerry, their sister and parents frequently met during the day to discuss resources and their conservation plans. This included, how to gain replenishments since all normal sources, such as regional distribution centers, are no longer available, nor are there any functional replenishment delivery trucks.

Their discussions lead to the Anderson family, and a few others of their local ilk, who are known to have practiced EMP survival preparation. They have stocked freeze-dried food with shelf lives of 10-25 years and other survival goods. Jerry remarked that the Anderson family may be under serious siege by looters seeking food, etc. As it developed, the Andersons may be ready to shoot any would-be burglars expected from the numerous new "Have Nots."

That afternoon, Hank and Jerry met with neighbors on both sides of their home. In comparing notes, one neighbor said his fridge is being used as an ice box and all remaining ice is about gone. They shared unfrozen food as it would soon become spoiled. Some of the meat was cooked using charcoal or wood on their outdoor, non-electric cookers.

Bottle water was a few days more in supply. However, the guy with the 11,000 gallon pool offered the neighbors to take bucket fulls and fill their bathtubs, toilets and other containers. Keep drinking water in the sinks. Then Jerry's Uncle Don from the hospital added that he knows of a way that pool water can be converted into into drinking water. This would be a good project for a few men to accomplish over several hours. However, this supposes we can get access to a small working generator (less than 5 kW) although there are other solutions. Here is how Don explained how it is done:

Get a plastic barrel, (wood will work if it doesn't leak) of at least 30 gallons. Get a hacksaw and a serrated edge knife.

(1) Cut the top off a plastic barrel with a knife and a hacksaw. Drill a half-inch drainage hole in the center of the bottom of the barrel.

(2- Line the bottom of the barrel with a cotton sheet.

(3)- Set the barrel on a stand. Use whatever works for the stand, such as sawhorses, cinder blocks or an old pallet, but remember you need to place

35

the water storage container(s) beneath it.

(4)- Shovel sand into the barrel, filling the bottom of the barrel with an even 2- inch thick layer.

(5)- Shovel charcoal into the barrel until you create a 4-inch layer. Periodically smash the charcoal with the shovel. Breaking up any large chunks and ensuring there is a compact layer.

(6)- Fill the barrel with alternating layers of sand and charcoal, repeating steps 3 and 4 until the barrel is filled about 25% from the bottom. Make the last layer sand, even if it means making the charcoal layer beneath it thinner. This creates a reservoir for pouring pool water into it to the filter.

(7)- Place one hose from the drainage pump into the pool, and the other hose into the reservoir at the top of the barrel filter. Put the first storage container underneath the stand . Turn the generator pump on.

(8)- Adjust the speed of the pump so it roughly matches the speed at which the filter processes the water. When the purified water container is full replace it with the next one. It would be helpful if cleaned, used 1-gallon plastic bottles are used as they weigh only 8 pounds when full.

When no generator or power is available and there is a slope down from the swimming pool, a gravity-fed approach can be used via siphoning action

----

Don Follow went on to say that we need to spread this word over all of Cantdo, or the larger developments, or at least in those areas where homeowners have a pool or even a smaller jacuzzi or hot tub.

As more neighbors gathered in the late afternoon conversation, one remarked that the Cantdo's single Dept of Agriculture guy told them there are about 80 head of cattle and 50 pigs in suburbia Cantdo. This is barely enough to feed Cantdo for about one week or 10 days at most, when rationed with other foods. Fortunately canned goods on all our shelves might extend this up to a month. But, then what?

This subject lead into the subject of Cantdo family "victory food gardens" as most everyone had during WWII. Even a

36

small amount of land, like 8' x 12' = 25 sq. ft. per person for a family of four, can grow several varieties of vegetables. Check the hardware and other stores (which may be closed) for seeds. While you are at it, get the old home canning book from the library (also probably closed) and pick up some jars and gaskets from the hardware store (probably closed, too) to can some food to carry many over the winter months. These may be hard to find.

The neighborhood gathering were reminded again of the above fortunate Anderson family and others like them who are survivalists, but whose lives may now be in jeopardy from desperate neighbor thieves. "Shame on us for not having seeds on hand or not having read books on EMP Survival", said Tommy Morgan, a 13 year-old boy scout present in the discussion. "So now you know our motto, 'Be Prepared'".

Then, Jerry remarked, "Finally, what about others from outside our neighborhood breaking into our homes to steal food and water. How many of us have guns and what is the ammunition supply? We have a lot of thinking and homework to do. Regrettably, we never took serious the Nuclear EMP warnings and publications over the past few years."

Thus, belated or not, Jerrry said, "Let us form a local group, both to ensure we know who we can trust and to determine the strength of our group resources." All agreed and the new session began inpromptu.

3.2 Bestville, VA (EMP Protected Town), Day 2

The radio announcements in Bestville spoke of a number of quick seminars some volunteers agreed to present over the coming week. The first involves the subject of telecommunications covering several priority aspects as they are vital to our ultimate survival and to permit us to optimize what we do over the forthcoming weeks and months – maybe even years. There will be time reserved for questions and answers during the seminars.

The first short one hour course given by Zack Thompson, a professor at the Bestville college, indicated a number of things we need to know on a regular basis. While some of these are in our indoctrination manuel that all residents have, they need to be given significant visibility now:

(1)- Our groceries, water, medications and fuel for our vehicles will run low unless certain planned replenishment actions come to pass in a timely manner. For example, since we have the map of the entire East Coast area that is dysfunctional, except for our Bestville and four other protected areas,, we need to identify the nearest cities of, say, 50,000 people or more on the periphery of the area having electricity and communications. This is achievable only via our satellite relay communications. Remember, these contacts are needed since one or more of these sources will become hubs for railroad and/or aircraft arriving here on a predetermined bases, as mentioned, with replenishments of food, medications and other provisions.

(2)- While our cell phones, ipads and the like work locally within our 75 sq. mile Bestville area, we need to devise a satellite or fiber optic link to central and west coast functional areas. Once we have that link we can make contact with many provision suppliers. But remember, nearly 100,000,000 Americans in the dysfunctional East Coast areas will be making very competitive demand for similar supplies. However they lack the communication means.

(3)- Although metro Washington, DC is in the same dysfunctional area, much of the pentagon, intelligence agencies and other Government Departments are EMP protected, but their nearby homes are not. So we need to make telecom contact there to ensure we get priority over other sectors vying for the same needs. This could become a logistical nightmare.

(4) Remember that Norfolk and Newport News are a home to a large sector of the US Navy fleet at any time. Since they are EMP protected, so will be their secured food, water and medication storage in adjoining areas. Thus, we must resume earlier established communications with contacts there.

(5) Now, listen carefully as this is the most important announcement reminder. We will have time for Q&A throughout the following discussions.

While it was hoped that many other neighboring villages, towns and cities would have had EMP protection by now, that is not the case. Since they know of our EMP protected town, we can expect some unfriendly visits. Therefore, we now pass out an orange band you are to wear immediately and at all times, to distinguish between Bestville citizens and others who may have entered here with unfriendly motives. Be Sure you don't tell others why you wear his band.

How can they enter? A few vehicles may still be functional. Or they may come by motor scooter, bicycle or in some cases by foot. The four main roads of entry and exit to Bestville will have an armed police officer assisted by one rotating volunteer to guard, question and interrogate visitors. This is not to imply that we will reject all visitors, though we will help them if we have more than sufficient supplies. This statement will be discussed later as we will have a few other volunteers watching other ways of entry.

The important matter of further discussion on project Zebra, on receiving pension funds and social security payments in a timely manner has not been forgotten. We will report on this with updates in the next two weeks.

3.3   Cantdo-Bestville, Lessons Learned, Day 2

The two town situations (especially Bestville) show the importance of both local and long distance communication. Locally, for intratown communication, a pair (+ maybe a spare) of short range (five mile) walkie talkies will greatly help in many situations where the cell phone system is dead.. Be sure to store them in a burned-out microwave oven (provides the necessary shielding) or other Faraday cage (a metal foil lined box on all six sides.

One of the more important needs early on, is to determine the periphery of the EMP impacted area. This gives the survivalist a planning base for replenishment supplies. This may be done with the assistance of a directory of radio AM, FM, short wave stations for US. If the survivalist's car radio is still working, the received radio AM stations ID, especially at night, is placed on a map. After locating, perhaps at least 10, connect them with a straight and nearby relief is identified (may be hundreds of miles. FM stations are limited to about 50 miles and none may be intercepted.

The shortwave radio will permit identifying more stations for drawing the periphery map. Unless the room or home is EMP protected, remember, to store the short wave or CB radio in a Faraday cage. All the above may be provided in the town from better equipped sources, but the survivalist needs to have his own short-wave radio.

Also, remember some satellite transmissions will be providing updated periphery maps of other protected areas and the peripheral ridge of the EMP impacted regions. This is helpful in our contacting relief sources to use our railroad siding and airstrip runway for vital replenishments.

It is quite possible that all this mapping of the periphery of the EMP damage may be provided as a service by some government agency to preclude the need for an individual to do this.

Basic EMP Survivalist

The EMP Survivalists group differs from both the Cantdo unprepared Town and Bestville - the EMP protected town types. Although they represent a small part of US population (perhaps 0.1%), EMP survivalists are found in every state and nearly every one of the 3,141 counties in USA.

EMP survivalists are independently operating and generally represent a collection of young families with the father under 35 years of age. Their motivation to spend time and their own money in EMP protection is in recognition of earlier-mentioned national EMP apathy and the fear of the consequences if not being prepared. This has been exacerbated by the fact that the US civil sector has done almost nothing in EMP protection and the survivalists perceive that there exists little evidence that the civil sector will be doing much anytime soon.

Their EMP survival preparation experience has developed a wealth of basic existence know-how. A browse through the Internet under "EMP Protection" key words or related search provides over 100 websites and advertisers and listings of items for sale. They generally plan to store one year supply of freeze-dry food, guaranteed to have a

Partial listing of candidate items EMP survivalist will seek to acquire.

Water	Electric & Electronics
Bottled	Light appliances
Canned	Flashlights
Well, hand pump	Batteries
Charcoal & sand filtered	Battery charger
Soft drinks	Shortwave radio
Brook or creek	Police Scanners
Food	CB radio
Canned food	Cell phone
Freeze dried	Batteries
Vegetable garden	Inverter
Cows and pigs	Ipad and/or ipod
Deer and squirrel	Microwave oven
Medications	**Computer & Peripherals**
Prescription drugs	**Candles and holders**
Vitimins	**Cooking**
Ointments	Propane heater
Pain killers	Propane storage tank
First aid kit	Charcoal
Splints and bandages	Box oven
Oxygen	Tin Can & Dutch ovens
Weapons and Ammo	Eating flatware
Pistols & revolvers	Kitchen utensils
Hunting rifles, shotguns	
Ammunition	
Matchetti	**Security**
Carving knives	Trip Alarms
Bow and arrows	Proximity alarms

42

25-year shelf life. They also plan on no electric power, although a few may even install a few solar panels to run a hope-fully EMP survived fan, a few electric lights, and electric powered tools.

The survivalist has accumulated articles and some books on plant identification, food preservation, first aid, disease control, outdoor survival, battery bank installation, wiring, solar and other alternative energy, medication, alternative medication, self defense weaponry, and other basics of self survival. Thus, some expertise should be developed in food supplies, wild foods and plants, water purification, communication and short-wave and CB radios, solar energy and wind turbines, heating small areas and cooking, security, medicine, first aid and sanitation.

Survivalists tend to prefer country living, preferably on a few acres, so that they can have a small crop supply of fruit and vegetables and be away from the crowded towns and cities, where they can be targets of desperate starving folks who seek to steal their vitals. They may also do hunting for deer, pheasant, turkey, wild boar, and rabbits, as available.

The above table lists most of what may be found therein. One of the more comprehensive books the reader may want to buy under $10 is *EMP Survival* by Larry and Cheryl Poole. It may be found on Amazon Books. A few others are:

• *Living off the Grid: a Simple Guide to Creating and maintaining a Self-reliant Supply of Energy, Water, Shelter and More*, by David S. Black, New York Skyhorse Pub, 2008.

• *A Field Guide to Edible Plants,* by Lee Allen Peterson, Peterson Field Guides, NY

Chapter 4

One Week Later

4.1 Cantdo, VA (EMP Unprotected Town), Week 1

Because several shots fired have been reported, some people are becoming desperate. Thus, Mayor Swanson formed a group of advisers, beyond the three that were introduced at the town gazebo meeting last week. They meet for about a half hour, daily, to report larger problem topics needing fixing, review the priorities, and make assignments. There would be five such groups: (1) food and drinking liquids, (2) medications, hospital and nursing-home, (3) fuel, vehicles and generators, (4) processing, location and burial of the dead, and (5) all other. Of course, with few exceptions, no one is any longer employed and all support is voluntary which makes the outcome and control nearly impossible or at least, very challenging..

The owner of Ames funeral home remarked that there were about 14 deaths last week, most coming from the hospital and nursing homes because of lack of oxygen and dialysis machine failures. The decedent cannot be embalmed or cremated as Ames and the two other funeral homes have no electric power. One suggestion has been made to move the decedent bodies out to the edge of the town trash dump, and make a common burial pit since the dirt is loose and the pit has to be dug by hand. (Remember no front loaders or backhoes are any longer functional).

Another employee of Ames remarked that they do not have a suitable vehicle that works. A third said there are a few horses in town and several flat wagons. Three volunteered to study the problem and return in two days with a best recommendation that can be implemented immediately. But, remember, this is hard to do since we have no working telephone, cell, computer or other communication.

Police chief, Mike Tolstoy reported that there have been three deaths from being shot due to home burglaries seeking food and water. Two more are dying from wounds, but there is no way to take them to the hospital, which can't help anyway because of other priority problems. For example, the hospital has no refrigeration and all such medications are being lost. Several of the staff is sleeping there due to exhaustion and lack of transportation. Their food supply is nearing depletion.

Bill Matovich, of the Fish and Wildlife Service, reported that the deer population is one source of food not estimated with the cows and pigs, now having been about 25% consumed. An ardent archer, Bill reports that he estimates there may be roughly 100 deer within 10 miles, and maybe many hundreds of rabbits. The game warden kicked in that fishing has already been increased tenfold. And perhaps 20 of the egrets, cranes and other bigger birds have been killed. Someone sarcastically joked, "Don't forget your pet dogs", which drew some nasty stares and snarls.

Bill Matovich then introduced Zig Campbell, a naturalists expert on wild edible plants. His masters thesis a few years ago was on how to help survive in the wilderness. Zig said, "It is important to get from the library, if it is still open or accessible, a plant identification book. Two examples are *A*

Field Guide to Edible Wild Plants, by Lee Peterson, or the U.S. Army *Illustrated Guide to Edible Wild Plants*. Remember, do not eat bitter tasting plants and milky juice plants. They may be poisonous, and, avoid wild mushrooms as risks are high.

"Your list should contain many fruits: wild grapes, strawberries, mulberries, raspberries, blueberries, blackberries. elderberries, apples, (not in the wild: oranges, tangerines, and grapefruit).

"Collect nuts from hickory, walnut and acorn trees, but roast to destroy parasites.

Among the edible plants are dandelions; Queen ante's lace; pigwood. chicory and purslane leaves, chickweed and wild onions.

" Don't forget frogs and turtles. Over 1,000 insects are eaten worldwide by humans including beetles, bees, wasps, ants, grasshoppers, crickets, moths and butterflies." Matovich concluded, "There are many more. The foregoing barely scratches the surface. So, get one of the above books cited ASAP."

Meanwhile, back at Hank and Jerry's home, Jennie, the younger sister, reported to her dad, Tom Drinkwell, and brothers that we are all beginning to smell through lack of bathing or showering. She stated, "There is no running water and, of course, there is no hot water as all electricity is gone." She also complained, "We are out of toilet paper, and I am tired of scooping out and emptying our toilet from human waste and dumping it in a neighborhood empty lot. I have already stepped in someone else's waste".

Since nearly all Cantdo working inhabitants have lost their

jobs following the EMP event, Jerry's father, Tom, suggested that the family is well overdue for a complete reassignment of duties. The banks in town are all closed, and besides cash is rapidly becoming worthless, they need to establish barter items to trade with others. And there must be some scheduling of hunting expeditions. Finely, they must consolidate this with the immediate neighbors and a few others as they too have similar needs. Here is the starter list of what Tom Harris has come up with, subject to family discussion and re consolidation with the neighbors:

List for Family Jobs and Chores Assignments

Task Identification	Hank	Jerry	Jenny	Dad	Mom
Hunting in woods for food	X	X			
Pool water purification	X	X			
Rainwater harvesting				X	
Fishing at Timberland Pond	X	X	X		
Get wood & fuel for cooking	X				
Food preparation & cooking			X		X
Food Garden Preparation		X			
Food Garden Maintenance			X		
Water carrying for bathing		X			
Inside household chores			X		X
Clothes sewing & Washing					X
Inside house maintenance				X	
Outside house chores & maintenance				X	
Dig pits in yard for garbage & waste	X	X			
Neighbor meeting & consolidating				X	X
Daily 15 min family meeting	X	X	X	X	X
ID and tagging bartering items				X	
Help out at church				X	X
Task Identification	Hank	Jerry	Jenny	Dad	Mom

Tom Drinkwell suggested that in addition to the starter list, we take a one day break for each of us to review, to add to the list any item taking more than two hours a week, and to replace the "X" in the list cells with an estimate of the hours per week it will take to accomplish. Then we meet in two days to

47

consolidate. Although the family is all cooperative the overhanging gloom was very apparent. And, yipes! This is only the first week..

4.2 Bestville, VA (EMP Protected Town), Week 1

The one daily a.m. Bestville broadcast station is now operated from 6:00 a.m. till midnight to keep all residents informed on post-EMP activities, news, assignments, warnings, critique and the like. However, town "classified information" is excluded since the broadcast might be picked up by other areas who may have listeners with ill-motives in mind. Thus, the daily mayor's meeting is still to be held at town hall grounds at 9:00 a.m. The mayor's messengers spread the word around of this and to be sure to wear your orange Bestville citizen ID bands.

At the mayor's meeting, Police Chief, Harold Schultz announced that Bestville, a town of low crime, is even lower as most all residents are extending helpful hands to fellow neighbors at these uncertain times. Also, since Bestville has a 98% EMP protection of its resident's homes and their workplaces and store fronts, there is no reason for EMP-generated "Have Nots" and the crime that would follow. For the few exceptions the positive neighborly, share attitude comes to the rescue. The local farmers are especially noted for their offers to help out and share some of the farm crop harvesting.

Regrettably, there was almost a skirmish at dusk yesterday when one of our resident neighborhood watch guards intercepted two intruders not wearing the orange Bestville ID arm bands. At gunpoint, our guard asked them from where they came. They replied from Jeston, a village about 15 miles away. He gave them a few provisions and told them to return immediately or they may get shot if not placed in jail as our town is off limits to intruders. Be sure to spread the word that unwelcomed out-of-town intruders risk being shot.

However, it is observed if visitors must communicate with Bestville, stop by guardpost #1 on Route 360 South. We will not discourage friendly solicited help exchange, but we must take care of our own first. A few of our locals exhibited concern that we need a more refined approach to arriving visitors. For example, what does the guard say if the visitor needs access to a dialysis machine as his hospital is dysfunctional? Obviously, we need a brief manual explaining what to do since this kind of preparation unfortunately escaped our broad post-EM manual preparation guide coverage.

At the mayor's meeting, the town supervisor, Tony Costello, announced that only about two percent of the population lost their jobs since the EMP event. Those individuals working mostly at motels depend upon out-of-town activities for their employment, such as tourism and a product imports and exports.

Regarding Project Zebra, mentioned earlier, the elderly inquired about their monthly social security and some asked about mail and parcel delivery. Regional Banker, Harold Johnson, replied that some local banking will remain in effect, but he is in disbelief if any USPS or postal deliveries will be resumed well into the unforeseeable future. This does not answer "What do Project Zebra folks use for cash", Johnson replied. I will arrange for a special reporting session on this within the week and hopefully include explicit options and bank transfers".

To close the mayor's meeting, Andy Moreland from the Bestville Hospital said he had a number of announcements to make about how the hospital was fairing. Briefly, it has all the necessary electricity, air conditioning and supplies. But, they may be running somewhat low in food and certain medications. However, they are in daily touch with distant hospital medical supply warehouses and small air carrier services to pickup and deliver to our airfield runway on some pretext of a weekly "services run." More information to follow

Thanks to the one large Bestville freeze-dry food and supply warehouse on Jefferson Avenue, survival food has about a year's supply on hand, provided there is no large run. They also have some of the more popular medications. All drawdowns of food must be paid for by cash at the time of purchase. No credit extended.

The above is beginning to illustrate the payoff and benefits of Bestville having been chosen as a major experimental EMP template preparation town. So the mayor's office made an assignment to three town folks to provide a near term and longer range recommendations on how it should help support neighboring Towns and Villages. One remarked that the Lord has been good to us and what might we do to help fulfill the Commandment of "Love Thy Neighbor as Thyself". Or, as Ken-nedy put it, "Ask not what America will do for you, but what together we can do for the freedom of man."

4.3 Cantdo-Bestville Lessons Learned, Week 1

Chapter lessons learned, underscores the penalty placed on all unprotected town families for not having a survival manual and a daily diary or daytimer record book. If the government, especially the 3,140 counties, do not have an EMP survival manual, the very least they can do is write a template for their town level using the many sources that are available on the Internet. Therein, it would be slanted and tailored for the town latitude and coastal or inland locations, near water or not, etc.

If the local County office does not get involved and there is none available at the State and Fed level, then it is possible that, where applicable, the project can be undertaken by a HOA (homeowners' Association). The chapter also illustrates how much is taken for granted in our modern way of life with its scores of accouterments such as water and funeral home, shown in the above example.

• Water	• Funeral Home
• Drinking Water	• Vehicle to Undertaker
• Bathing	• Electricity for Cremation
• Showering	• Electricity for Lighting
• Toilet Flushing	• Electric Signs
• Dish Washing	• Air Condit. for Services
• Clothes Washing	• Hearse for Funeral Transport
• Watering Lawns	• Backhoe to dig trench
• Pressure Washing	• Motor to lower casket
	• Vehicle to Return

Any book for EMP Protection should have the material as chapters and some of the more technical material included as appendices. One such template may look a bit like the following:

Residential Guide to Become EMP Aware and Protected

(Note: this guide may be broken into a few parts for Homeowners, Commercial and Industrial, Public Works and Electric Utilities.

- Front Material
- Chapter 1, About (EMP) the Electromagnetic Pulse
- Chapter 2, About Solar Flares
- Chapter 3, Life without Electric Power
- Chapter 4. Life without both Power and Electronics
- Chapter 5, Lifestyles with and without EMP Preparation
- Chapter 6, What the EMP Survivalists Do
- Chapter 7, Backup Power and EMP Protection
- Chapter 8, EMP Protection for Small Group of Families
- Chapter 9, EMP Protection for Homeowner's Association
- Chapter 10, EMP Protection for Villages
- Chapter 11, EMP Protections for Towns
- Chapter 12, EMP Protection for Cities
- Chapter 13, Financing EMP Protection Programs
- Chapter 14, EMP Protection of Commercial Buildings
- Chapter 15, EMP Protection of Industrial Buildings
- Chapter 16, EMP Protection of Solar Farms
- Chapter 17, EMP Options for Getting Involved in EMP Protection
- Appendices

Lacking a working vehicle provides severe constraints on not going to and from shopping malls, medical doctors, hardware stores, gasoline station, church and the like. Unless and until, the auto manufacturers have a few of their vehicles tested at Dayton T. Brown or other MP test facility, and report to the public, the public will not really know what to expect re probability of vehicle becoming dysfunctional or garage shielding needed, etc.

Perhaps, one of the worst situations following an EMP burst for an unprotected town is the almost certain loss of a paying job. No transportation to or from home to work; no lighting at the place of employment; no air conditioning; no flushing toilets; no computer; no cell phones, etc. The change in lifestyle is so gross as to question the entire concept of EMP survivalists. Yet, survivalists state clearly that they are going the natural survival route because the government has done essentially nothing. One day when the first event happens, the whole country will go berserk as the demands for food, water, medicines, gasoline, ammo will totally overload the supply. But, that is just what it will take to "Wake up America", and make it all happen.

Chapter 5

One Month Later

5.1 Cantdo, VA , (EMP Unprotected Town), Month 1

At their daily meeting, Mayor Swanson introduced Dr. Blemming, who summed up that our Cantdo town population was about 10,500. In a normal month we have about 15 deaths and 17 births. However, one month after EMP, we have over

Reaons for Death in USA, 2009 Records

Women Reason for Death	%	Men Reason for Death	%
Heart disease	24	Heart disease	25.2
Cancer	22.2	Cancer	24.4
Stroke	6.3	Injuries	6.2
Chronic Lower respirtory	5.9	Chronic Lower respiratory	5.3
Alzhalimer's disease	4.5	Stroke	4.3
Injuries	3.5	Diabetics	2.9
Diabetics	2.8	Suicide	2.4
All Else	31.8	All Else	29.3

200 deaths so far including some infants who couldn't make it to the hospital or clinic. No midwives nor helpers could be found. "The death population is mostly elderly sector from lack of medication and physicians care. In this respect, examine what people die from in normal

Risk Rate vs. Blood Pressure

Blood Pressure	Risk Rate*
115-75	Normal
135-85	2X
155-95	4X
175-105	8X

*Applies as multiplier to the normal risk of Heart Attacks or Stroke

Novartis Pharmaceuticals

times in USA as shown in placard table I now hold up for all to see," said Dr. Blemming.

"Now, one month later, the Cantdo hospital and a few of the local clinics are almost closed for business. No electricity; no medication requiring refrigeration; no air conditioning; no lights, oxygen nor dialysis machines, etc. Without any functional MRIs, Cat Scanners, or X-Ray machines, and few attending physicians, nurses and other helpers, Cantdo population will now start dying in larger percentages. For example, about 30% of decedents normally die from heart attacks and strokes. When this is compared to a person with increasing blood pressure, his or her death rate increases exponentially. This is shown by my assistant holding up the second placard above", stated Dr. Blemming.

In his verbal report, police chief Mike Tolstoy said, "Those killed from home burglaries are strongly on the rise. A few remarked that they no longer have ammo and Spikes Gun Shop said they are almost out of the popular 9 mm and shotgun shells. They already had a shop break in and some hand guns were stolen in the first week."

"Arson seems to be on the rise as are suicides. Unfortunately, no fire trucks are working so that we just hope for the rains and less wind. Community shelters are also very heavily attended and soon will run out of supplies, not the least being food and water."

A neighborhood cook-out "feast" was to be planned before the hunters returned. Fortunately, there is still some hand butane igniters available to start the fires and most of the fuel is cut wood as nearly all the charcoal is gone. Cigarettes are no more and smokers have lost or misplaced most of their hand lighters.

The hunters, Hank and Jerry Drinkwell and their friend returned from hunting with two deer and three rabbits to their favor. One deer was skinned and disembowel at the party grounds while some others looked on. One of the fire pits, prepared for the party, was converted to process (cook) the deer. The party continued on with blessings for better times to come amongst all the gloom and doom. Just wait till the gathering is over and all return to the scary and uncertain future awaiting them. Some people are beginning to give up hope.

One couple joined the party late to announce that they bicycled over near Deep Creek development when a helicopter circled several times and then landed in an open field, near the gate house. Many of the residents ran to the chopper to find out what was happening. The pilot told them they are from Chesapeake Naval Base and are instructed to survey the areas and report back. When he told them he also had several medications and some food and water on board, a few nutty desperadoes in the group immediately rushed and overtook the pilot, knocking him to the ground. They fought over the boxes and two including the pilot were shot in the ensuing fight. Then a sad recognition set in as (1) no report was yet unfolded regarding the expanse of the EMP outage or (2) no one knew how to operate the helicopter to fly wherever.

The next day, Hank and Jerry critiqued the helicopter incident and realized that there is some active life at the military air and ship bases on coastal regions, especially on the Chesapeake and around Newport - Hampton - Norfolk, about

57

180 miles away from Cantdo. They also reasoned (guessed) that those neighboring areas may have been spared the EMP aftermath or at least with boats and ships can go afar to gain provisions. After all, an aircraft carrier sports 4,000 swabbies alone. So, why not go there and find out. But how?

Hank and Jerry also spent some time on pausing and reflecting on why they have not considered moving out of Cantdo long before now. There are some known villages that are believed to have partly become EMP protected and therefore enjoy some aspects of lifestyles in contrast to Cantdo. The helicopter event served to remind them that it is time for serious reflection. Were it not for family and a few friends, and the extreme difficulty of travel, they would have been gone long before now.

Jerry said, "Ken Atwater, the 1980 Pontiac hardtop guy, must know of his other fortunate older car owners who we might convince to join us or borrow their vehicle for a consideration in sharing the outcome".

Jerry then added "With all the scores of cars stuck in various roads and streets, their gas tanks must still have quantities of fuel. Using Ken's Pontiac or our bicycles with a trailing small wagon we can go to Pep Boys, NAPA or Sears."

Hank interrupted, "We can break in if the store is not open and bring back at least twelve, 5-gallon plastic cans for storing 60 gallons of petrol. This would get us over 420 miles for a round trip to Norfolk and other areas." Hank concluded, "However, fuel alone would weigh 450 pounds and waste petrol with the load, so why not have six 5-gallon cans full and the rest empty for possible future filling elsewhere."

Conclusion: after arranging for borrowing an old car in fairly good repair and getting the gas cans, they will get a detailed map of Virginia and plan the trip carefully. Unfortunately with no computer, they cannot use map websites. Food, water, money, other provisions and time to plan the trip would be needed.

But, as it developed their father overheard their discussions and cut in with, " Hey, guys, why not bring your ideas to Mayor Swanson's office and discuss them. He could arrange to get the car, gas cans, plus a letter of introduction from his office that you can show any Marshall stopping you about your mission."

In fact, their dad went on to say "There are several logistic facts like extent of region with EMP aftermath, when help might arrive, etc. that we need to know here in Cantdo. What say you?"

They decided to go to bed and discuss it in the morning. But, Jerry and Hank weren't convinced about "when help will arrive and other wishful considerations."

In another meeting held locally the same day with about fourty concerned Cantdo citizens at the local closed college library, erstwhile real estate broker, Harold Swanson, was preparing for a long awaited presentation regarding Project Zebra.

Swanson began "I welcome you folks to this long awaited meeting resulting from many requests to me from you as individuals. This to let you know in advance that most of what I have to say is not good news but does provide some hope and expectations if certain measures can be taken after a most catastrophic EMP incident last month."

Swanson continued, "The Bronxville Evening News ran an article on April 23, 2013 Times Herald, '*An Almost Economic and Financial Market Loss.*' *'Today*, the stock market almost lost about $200 billion dollars for a few minutes on a Twitter-hacked rumor of a White House explosion, before correcting. This resulted from many software account trigger, sell-order programs having a loss mitigation, safety protection action."

Swanson added, "Suppose the rumor had been a sudden EMP burst instead, in which the electric grid went down along with all RAM and backup memory that became dysfunctional. Even flash memory was burnt out by being connected to a mother board. All the stock brokerage houses, banks, insurance companies, retirement funds, annuity records and the like back-up memory were lost. Are your equity records in the hands of others EMP non-protected institutions? Can you prove your loss to the institutions who have also become dysfunctional ? Are your life savings gone in a heartbeat?"

Swanson continued, "The above true story of the April 23, 2013 stock market event was self correcting because of software escape protections. Today, the real EMP event was a month ago and all retirement funds, savings accounts, annuities peculiar to the EMP impacted area will be lost in their records, a few exceptions notwithstanding. Social security records, however, are also housed in EMP unaffected areas, so records are not lost."

Harold Swanson added, "However, the problem gets even bigger. How are the monthly retirement funds, annuities, even social security checks going to be delivered (or electronic transfer) to Cantdo retirees when there is no mail delivery because of dysfunctional vehicles and no gas stations, extremely little communication, no Internet and so on. Thus, all your monthly subsistances are no longer possible and records may never be re-created."

Upon hearing this, mass bedlem broke out at the meeting with some of the audience fainting and screaming, cursing and the like. Two CPR attempts were initiated. The scene quickly got out of control and Harold Swanson immediately realized he had committed a catastrophic no-no by not having told individuals or families separately and in a far more couched manner. Too late now! How to overcome this?

5.2 Bestville, VA (EMP Protected Town), Month 1

At Mayor Henderson's daily "classified meeting" he noticed a decidedly energetic, upbeat and thankful gathering as Bestville was nearly prospering throughout the somewhat otherwise gloom and doom national East Coast, post-EMP situation.

He announced that Virginia Governor Maxwell's office has communicated with the few Virginia EMP protected Towns including Bestville about a proposed flight trip to visit us next week. Three folks would be coming. The mission would be twofold, namely:

(1)- Learn as much as possible about how our own town, Bestville, is faring in the post-EMP event. They want to know all the good, bad and indifferent news, and especially lessons learned. They also wanted a copy of Bestville's daily logs for further study and additives so that others back home and elsewhere in USA can benefit.

(2)- They will conduct a several hour seminar over the local radio conveying how the other EMP protected towns are doing. This will end with an early prediction of what the near-term future appears to offer and when things may get better.

Central and West Coast USA are in good shape as they did not have an EMP burst. But most of the East Coast is in deep trouble. Thanks to the few experimental towns like Bestville, hope is on the rise in some sectors. But the vast majority of other areas have required the National Guard be called to subdue riots and disorders. All the humanitarian services elsewhere are overloaded trying to help out and are now at marginal performance levels.

The National tone is, "If only we became more prepared during 2007-2013 period instead of our apathy, lethargy and other preoccupation, things would have been very different."

The Governor's office air trip to Bestville, also had another hidden mission. Using Bestville as a temporary home, they will set up a small bastion of 25 National Guard on the outskirts of Bestville. The purpose is to distibute water food, medications, clothing and other essentials to desperate regions within about 120 miles of Bestville.

Most of the goods deliveries would be made by restoration vehicles (high payload small trucks). The Guard would also be used to help control the rapid increase of crime outside of Bestville. The Have-Nots are growing, independently, to a non coordinated, small army of serious trouble, robberies, fights, murders and, in some cases, nearing total anarchy.

Mayer Henderson said. "The Governor's office advises that the best way to deal with increasing crime, is to first provide more food and water, and selected medications and a functional clinic (if not a small hospital) capable of X-Raying and Cat Scanning, supported by two resident injury and surgical physicians, two nurses and two ANs. With that in mind, Bestville may receive outside support to convert or construct a hospital with at least 40 beds to help the outlining areas not capable of any clinical support, While potentially controversial to Bestville residents, this has some very compelling arguments".

Mayer Henderson concluded, "I will keep Bestville residents fully informed. In the meantime I will assign two of my office helpers to canvass about 100 Bestville residents to get their views and comments for feedback to the Governor's office.

Finally, banker Rochester reported the following about Project Zebra on retirement pensions, social security, mail and postal deliveries"

"Regarding social security monthly and disability checks, East Coast originating mail services have been handed over to a major hub at Cleveland, OH for government mail only, including monthly Social Security checks. Non-Government mail originating or receiving in the EC EMP region has been "temporarily" suspended. Meanwhile, Fed EX had been contracted to handle this. However, this is available only to EMP protected towns like Bestville, military bases, most Washington, DC government operations, and other undisclosed classified locations.

For private pension plan holders, individual sources have been contacted to use the Fed-Ex Cleveland delivery service. To be sure you have not been left out, use Satellite Phone Service to contact, Fed-Ex, Tempo USPS mail Services, Pension Dept., 1220 Street, Cleveland Ohio, 44101. The big news, however, is that all heretofore mail of EMP protected town pension and SS checks are being changed to be done electronically by bank transfer. Regrettably, and a major goof indeed, is that unprotected towns will receive an unknown distribution with many, if not most, never reaching their intended targets!

Repeating the last sentence for emphasis, retirement moneys from pension funds, retirement sources, annuities, social security, and the like will most likely never reach those towns that have been exposed to an EMP burst. Recipients almost immediately have little to no funds to consider. Some will argue that this is academic as money will rapidly become worthless as things are bought by bartering, anyway. Thank God, that we are Bestville, an EMP protected town.

5.3 Cantdo-Bestville, Lessons Learned, Month 1

The trip from the Virginia Governor's office was a great morale booster and generator for three main things learned from the new 40-bed additional tempo hospital to be built from the Old Mill River Structure at Bestville. The Project Zebra Postal and retirement mail transfer/replacement, and the proposed starter template EMP protection book are well overdue additives. They should be great for awareness and planning.

Fortunately and fortuitously, the Old Mill River structure is on the far end of the adjoining hospital grounds. Since it is a well built structure, the ability to upgrade the construction, adding many partitions, two elevators, etc. is much quicker and at a lower cost than starting anew. Another approach, is that there is additional structure to upgrade to 85 beds. If ever needed, the grounds can accommodate more than 200 beds if it should ever become a regional hospital.

Reminder: This hospital update is primarily to service non-Bestville residents up to 120 miles, since Bestville, being EMP protected, has been and remains self sufficient, except for the need of periodic basic replenishments. Once Phase 2 (runs from 2015 to 2023) of the USA EMP Protection Plan becomes implemented (see *"EMP – Protect Family, Homes and Community"*), except for regional medical sector specialty emphasis, hospitals and clinics should serve their own local needs.

While the main lesson learned is that every village or town should have its own EMP protected clinics (with X beds) or a hospital. In the final analysis, all towns should be so EMP protected with operational backup solar rooftops. This also means that in time the electric grid system will slowly shift from a network of power generating/distribution hubs to millions of solar rooftops with some having adjoining mini solar farms for taller buildings. The roll of the electric grid may slowly and partly shift to serving over 200,000, electric-vehicle charging stations in USA located at other than homes, such as, shopping malls, Well-Marts and House Depots, restaurants, theaters, churches, hotels and motels, stadiums, etc.

Project Zebra, discussed in a previous chapter, addresses how to deal with delivery of retirement and pension funds, social security payments, annuity payments, reverse-mortgage pay-ments, etc. All payments are made by originating sources to the recipients designate banks in EMP protected areas, via satellite communications. Non EMP protected areas will receive no service as there becomes no way to serve locations without electricity, electronics and many operational vehicles.

The USPS, regarded by many to be an obsolescent service, is perceived by many to become discontinued in a few to several years. Fed X and UPS will pick up any slack along with bank transfers

----

The previous Chapter Section, *4.3 Cantdo – Bestville Lessons Learned, Week 1* addressed the needed and proposed, government issued, *"A Survival Manual on Community EMP Protection"*. This manual becomes a template from which other derivative manuals should be adopted or five different apps or entities:

- An EMP Survival Manuel for Hamlets and Villages
- An EMP Survival Manuel for Towns
- An EMP Survival Manuel for Small Cities
- An EMP Survival Manuel for Homeowners Associations

- Methodology and Techniques for EMP Shielding, Bonding, Grounding, Surge Suppression and Filtering

A series of slide shows should be prepared for use by educational and training organizations, both for the general public and for professionals. They cover the above five application manuals and will ensure that many times more population will participate via seminars and webinars than will read the manuals, since people have become lazy and are much more inclined to watch videos and shows. In this regards, slide shows can beget the corresponding seminars, which in turn, beget making live videos with questions and answers added during seminars. Also, it is easier to update and distribute videos and slide shows

Chapter 6

Three Months Later

6.1 Cantdo, VA , (EMP Unprotected Town), Month 3

As an update to the Drinkwell brothers plan to have an expedition to Newport News two months earlier, they did follow their dad's advice and engage Mayor Swanson's office. Therein, they received an affidavit for their travels and their mission "on behalf of Cantdo" seeking support from the Naval installations or others. Hank and Jerry also got their plastic gas cans and other materials and goods for the 210-mile trip.

A Naval helicopter landed at Cantdo bearing news and some provisions, plus Jerry Drinkwell. Regrettably, Hank, Jerry's brother had died from food poisoning and their vehicle was stolen. The helicopter pilot reported that the demands on the several Naval basis has turned out to dispersing food, water and goods to scores of towns and cities along most of the East Coast and several hundred miles inland. The pilot apologized for the infrequent visit from their Naval base, but their survival replenishment mission is severely overloaded.

The pilot did provide some encouragement that the Seaport at Charleston, SC has been receiving steam locomotives from Europe and Australia so that major railroads can distribute replenishments to the hundreds of towns and cities in Eastern USA. The Naval helicopter also contained 20 short-wave, battery-operated radios so Cantdo can keep in touch with the rest of USA and Canada and gain some expectations about survival relief. The radios also have hand-cranked generators to ensure power for being kept informed when the batteries were consumed.

Another major meeting took place at the town gazebo at 10:00 a.m. There Mayor Swanson and several of the close working groups reported the following:

Scores of premature deaths from water and food starvation and from food poisoning. It is estimated that about one third of the Cantdo population has died from several causes especially from salmonella breakouts and other epidemics. There are no undertaker or funeral services. Decedents are buried in three main areas: large open pits in nearby Saulton woods, the city dump, and at the cemetery.

Most horses, and all cattle and pigs were gone. Discussions did turn to killing pets for food. It is estimated that half the population have already killed their pets for food and to save feeding them as well. House burglaries are routine. Most other stores were not raided as word gets around that they have already had break-ins and been picked over.

Almost no contact with neighboring towns or elsewhere with almost no telecom and travel vehicles, no airplane, train or bus are operational.

There were some discussions about eating those of recent death with no disease. Ammunition for self protection was running low. Emergency services are no longer available.

Hope was all but gone as there was little expectations of any relief vehicles or prospects. Suicides and shootings were on the increase.

Meanwhile, back at the Drinkwell home, they were comparing progress on their Task Assignment list. Since, Hank had regrettably perished as reported before. The list has grown and there are fewer family members to help out.

Jenny reported that she has a gigantic tooth ache and there exists no dentists to help out especially since the dentist has no electricity. Having had an earlier root canal operation, the family was at loss what to do other than tooth extraction. Maybe Dr. Smallwood, the dentist, could be found to see if he has any novacain or can help out in some way, if he hasn't died too. However there is no operational vehicle nor any gasoline fuel available. Can't call him on cell or telephone since neither works. All very discouraging and demoralizing.

So Tom Drinkwell, Jenny's father, described what options exist for tooth removal default. First, they still have some Advil tablets in their pantry closet. Start by taking two. Remember they are not an anesthesia. Tooth extraction is not an enjoyable experience as it is, and will be less so in a long-term survival situation with no power and limited supplies as we have here. Unlike baby teeth, a permanent tooth is unlikely to be removed simply by wiggling it out with your (gloved) hand or tying a string to it and the nearest doorknob and slamming the door. Also, be aware that pieces of jaw bone that are very firmly attached to the root of the tooth can sometimes come out during the extraction. Tom and Jerry will immediately try to locate a doctor or dentist who can help out

----

In a more positive vein, two of the mayor's group leaders reported:

(A)- The vegetable garden started almost three months ago was a major success and had high priorities for survival, but produce was too early to harvest, which would start in a few weeks.

About 30 families moved out to Cantdo's suburbia where 14 farms are located. They were housed and slept in barns and other farm shelters. They helped the farmers in expanding the vegetable farming, and restarting cattle and pig farming from the mated pairs delivered by the helicopter pilot. Fuel was obtained from EMP disabled abandoned vehicles as mentioned earlier. While the newer tractor microprocessor's were burned out, the older tractors still worked. Enough to till the fields (and the older backhoes were used to dig burial pits for the deceased)

(B)- The earlier discussion on how to develop drinking water from swimming pools was a major reason for otherwise fewer deaths. There were a few hundred pools located in Cantdo that carried out the process discussed in an earlier chapter. While cooking and filter charcoal had run short, they learned how to make charcoal from selected woods – sometimes an arduous undertaking. This is done in the following manner:

Materials needed: A propane heater (usually available at hardware stores for $35) with propane gas tank, a charcoal chimney (stove pipe 4-12" in diameter) and with internal can (one to 5-gallon paint can) somewhat smaller in diameter containing three holes punched in the top, and channel locks for removing the hot can containing the wood pieces to be converted to charcoal) . A supply of wood with preferences for pine or willow.

(1)- Place the charcoal chimney on top of the burner and connect the burner to the propane gas supply.

(2)- fill the empty paint can with several pieces of broken up wood with larger pieces around the outside wall. Put the lid with holes back on the paint can and place inside the chimney.

71

(3)- Ignite the burner (hand igniter or cigarette lighter) and cook for about 1-1/2 hours. Cook at a low-medium level – not too fast or it won't work.

(4)- When white smoke comes out the three holes that is a sign of dry distillation in which steam and resin in the wood are being cooked.

(5)-When the steam turns to a grayish-brown color, shortly thereafter, flames will come out the three holes in the paint can – a sign that the process is nearly over. The oils are burned off.

(6)- Remove the inner paint can with the tongs and turn it upside down on th dirt ground to block oxygen from getting therein. Leave to cool down.

(7)- Break up the charcoal wood into small pieces. Place the contents into a larger container for later use.

(8) Note: There are other somewhat similar ways to make larger quantities of charcoal not discussed here.

6.2 Bestville, VA (EMP Protected Town), Month 3

Mayor Henderson's 7:30 a.m. morning meeting, is now only conducted on the radio station at Bestville where it can reach more listeners than previously at the town square. The time is earlier to enable Bestville employees to hear their office presentation before leaving for work. A repeat broadcast is made at 7:00 p.m. for those missing the morning event.

Police Chief Schultz reported the latest news involves the middle of the night break-in at Well-Mart's Supercenter. This operation is normally closed from midnight to 5:00 a.m. because of the electricity curfew to allow less drain on the solar batteries and generator gas consumption. Apparently, several burglars smashed through the food center entrance driving a narrow truck between the steel guard posts and then crashed through the double sliding doors.. They cleaned the canned fish and canned meat shelves of about $4,500 in goods - all in a few minutes and then exited in their truck right back out the entranceway and into the night, with the store sirens blaring, and emergency outside lighting notwithstanding.

The burglars apparently escaped via a residential region, probably off Howard Street, but none of the four guarded Bestville highway gates reported any activity. So the burglars may still be hidden in some garage within Bestville. All this is very strange since Faramville residents are not suffering from food starvation. Therefore the intruders may be from a location other than Bestville. Remember our orange arm bands. Anyone learning any information, please report to the police at satellite: 434-345-2345 ASAP.

Chief Schultz then turned the discussion back over to the mayor. Mayer Henderson then remarked, "Tuesday is the 3rd

73

month anniversary of the EMP event. Bestville is very fortunate to have about 95% employment since it is estimated from other broadcast receptions that non EMP-protected towns have less than 5% employment and their death rate is very high. Our thanks go to many things which contribute to our advanced EMP protection efforts including our prayers to the Lord.

"One which received little recognition early on, is our 4,000 foot dirt runway landing strip. Last month a C-17 Globemaster III made its first landing. Its single-flight payload limit is 85 tons (170,000 pounds) with conceptually enough food to feed the entire town of Bestville for one week or to replenish our warehouse for about one month. The tanker version of the Globemaster can carry 25,000 gallons of gasoline, enough fuel to permit most vehicles, that are used to get to and from work, to function for nearly one month."

Mayor Henderson then introduced Tony Costello, Town Supervisor. Tony said, "I would like to first add to the mayor's remarks that the Governor has authorized Bestville to receive steel mats to place over the dirt air runway, the type used by the military in captured war zones. These mats will reduce accidents from runway potholes due to rain water washout.

"A bastion was set up at Guardpost #1 at Route 360 South town limits for a small 30-unit national guard. Some emergency trucks will be flown in together with a few riot control vehicles and food vans as the state protection and delivery of food and other supplies out to about 120 miles of Bestville. The guard will be setting up a small, EMP-protected solar-PV farm on five acres to provide enough power to handle all their operations."

Costello concluded, "With financial help from Virginia, Bestville has been chosen to set up a second hospital to care for the selected (mostly younger) folks from other neighboring areas where no functional hospitals or clinics exist. Details will be presented tomorrow.

Finally, John. Garwood, Director of our County Economic Development Office, reported the latest findings of their outreach committee, to wit, "As you all know, Bestville was chosen, in a tight competition, as one of a few Towns on the East cost of 18 states from Maine to Florida and west to the Application Mountains. Although we are paying for 85% of our own support, Bestville received some from the state of Virginia and Fed protection. Collectively we represent less than 0.05% (one per 2,000) of the area population."

We have long standing plans to convert the Mills Culture Center into a combination of seminar and education/training center and museum focusing on the entire EMP subject of EMP Protection. This is part of a National plan to make USA citizens more aware of EMP and the many options for EMP protection from small family groups up to large towns of 50,000 people. In one sense, we are following the boy scout memo of "Be Prepared". Truly, this is too late for the recent EMP event, but the Center will be visited by thousands and very active in training in preparation of EMP protection if/when another strikes. More to follow tomorrow."

Garwood said, I have a quick, human-interest story that may be of interest to all. Yesterday afternoon, Carroll Smallvine from Bestville's Northport estates said that every time she touched her new aluminum kitchen window with one hand to open or close the window, and the other hand was on the sink faucet for extended reaching support, she got an electrical shock. A call for help to a neighboring electrician disclosed that a screw to secure the window frame to the wall frame pierced an inside electric cable insulation as well and put 120 volts on the window frame. So when Carroll touched both the window and the faucet at the same time, she got shocked. The fix was simple. Use a shorter, but wider screw which would not reach to the inside wall routed electric circuit wiring.

6.3 Cantdo-Bestville, Lessons Learned, Month 3

Two big things learned during this three month period: (1) The importance of protecting and preserving hospitals and clinics, and (2) Even big Globemaster food and supplies replenishment aircraft can land and take off in a 4,000 foot runway.

(1)- A tooth extraction is a big painful episode with no electricity, no dentist, no anesthesia, no tools, no sanitation, etc. Not much help from the EMP survivalists. So, hospitals and clinics must receive extra attention and funding for area EMP protection. That's why the planned offer from the Virginia Government's office provided extra support out to 120 miles from already protected Bestville, that is self sufficient except for periodic replenishments of medications and other supplies.

First a few stats on Hospitals:

Total Number of All U.S. Registered * Hospitals: 5,724
Number of U.S. Community ** Hospitals:4,973
Number of Non-Gov., Not-for-Profit Community Hospitals: 2,903
Number of Investor-Owned (For-Profit) Community Hospitals: 1,025
Number of State and Local Government Community Hospitals: 1,045
 Number of Federal Government Hospitals: 208
 Number of Nonfederal Psychiatric Hospitals: 421
 Number of Nonfederal Long Term Care Hospitals: 112
 Number of Hospital Units of Institutions
 (Prison Hospitals, College Infirmaries, Etc.) 10
Total Staffed Beds in All U.S. Registered * Hospitals: 924,333
 Staffed Beds in Community** Hospitals: 797,403
Total Admissions in All U.S. Registered * Hospitals: 36,564,886
 Admissions in Community** Hospitals" 34,843,085
Total Expenses for All U.S. Registered * Hospitals :$773,546,800,000
 Expenses for Community** Hospitals : $702,091,034,815
Number of Rural Community** Hospitals: 1,984
Number of Urban Community** Hospitals: 2,989
Number of Community Hospitals in a System *** 3,007
Number of Community Hospitals in a Network *** 1,535

Summary:
>   Total USA Hospitals: 15, 670
>   Total USA Population: 315,000,000
>   Population per Hospital: 20,102

>   Total Number of Hospital Beds: 1,721,736
>   Average Beds per Hospital: 183
>   Population per Hospital Bed: 184

The existing building conversion route forr a new hospital was chosen to serve the peripherial area installation at Bestville. The estimate population of the 120 mile radius surrounding Bestville is about 212,000 people. Assuming all hospitals are dysfunctional following the EMP burst, then 212,000/20,102 pph = 10 hospitals are required to serve the area. So, the Virginia Governor.s office has underestimated the load by a factor of 10. The entire project must be re-evaluated in terms of the hospital density and people served. This will not be done here.

(2)- The fact that a huge Globemaster III air cargo can carry a load of 85 tons into a landing strip of 3,500 feet is a God-send to all impacted areas with a 4,000 foot dirt runway covered by light steel mats. Liquids, food, medications, gasoline and other provisions, delivered to a consuming area in a timely manner, is a life-line to lifestyle having a degree of survival well above that planned by the EMP survivalist. This opens up an otherwise logistical nightmare into an era of delivery not possible or practical by land vehicles.

Chapter 7

One Year After

7.1 *Cantdo, VA (EMP Unprotected Town), Year 1*

Arrangements were set for a gathering in memory of the first anniversary of the EMP event. About 1,000 of the town's population remain or 10% of the original 10,500 population, have survived. The survivors are mostly the young and healthy who have also developed an enormous street smarts by learning, pragmatically, what works and what does not. Unfortunately, without the Internet and other sources on survival, the population was ill equipped to deal with a major disaster, let alone an EMP event. How sad, in retrospect, that Cantdo took the entire EMP warnings for years as though nothing like this would ever happen.

The death rate would have been much greater were it not for the many developed food gardens, both large and small, and both inside Cantdo and its outskirts. Thanks to the railroad siding, nearly all external replenishments (but far-far under needs) arrived by rail later via wood-burning steam engines. The 4,000-foot dirt landing strip was never installed as in EMP-protcted towns. However, much of the survival credit goes to the small body of family EMP survivalists who were well equipped but constantly harassed by the Have Nots.

In retrospect, one sad thing about Cantdo, is that the concept of "Vital Replenishments" was never addressed (other than locally) when it had opportunities to reflect upon earlier consideration of some degree of EMP protection. No dirt runway was chosen as planners assumed there was no communications with survival. Yet, the unsuspected earlier helicopter arrival at Cantdo brought a 500 watt transmitter with solar panel to let the rest of the country know about its status. With this and the several protected short-wave radios, a closed loop of communications is possible re deliverance of vitals (freeze-dried fool, popular medications, hunting shotgun ammo) by a Globemaster discussed in sections 6.2 and 6,3 in this faction book.

So with all the above food gardens and plantings, food was no longer very scarce, but then remember, 90% of the population of Cantdo had also perished. Canning could not be done as few knew how to do it and there were no canning jars or jar gaskets to be found. Meat was no more except for occasional squirrel, rabbit, possum or raccoon. All else had been over hunted in the surrounding areas by Cantdo hunt parties who often brought back no catch. Similarly birds and fish were few and far between.

The death rate from starvation and disease were dominant. Many more were from hepatitis, injuries and some amputations at the residue of the hospital, ill-equipped to handle more than becoming a morgue. However, the two older generators, had finally been retired as there was no more fuel. More than a thousand gallons of gasoline had been siphoned from stalled vehicles within ten miles. The fuel was put into container cans and brought to the hospital for generator use for limited lighting, surgery, and other critical medical uses.

7.2 Bestville, VA (EMP Protected Town), Year 1

Ironically, Bestville was planning for a one year, EMP anniversary gathering at its new updated Mill River EMP Convention Center and Museum. More than 70 exhibit booths, 4,500 participants and eleven, 1-3 hour EMP seminars lead the main affairs for two days. Most sources are from outside Bestville and the demised East Coast EMP afflicted region.

Little Bestville is being placed on the USA map for EMP activity as the first pilot project to become greatly expanded in the future. The following eleven seminars, projected on a giant 18-foot screen in two halls cover the following subjects:

(1)- An Introduction to EMP - an Historical Overview
(2)- Discussion about EMP vs. Solar Flare Threats
(3)- Contrasting EMP Lifestyles – A Tale of Two Towns
(4)- Lessons Learned from EMP Survivalists
(5)- One EMP Template: A Major Roll for All Economic
       Development Offices.
(6)- How to EMP Shield and Protect Detached Homes, and
       Test Compliance Certifications
(7)- How to Pay for all Costs and Who Pays and ROI
(8)- How to EMP Shield and Protect Commercial and
       Industrial Buildings.
(9)- How to EMP & Solar Flare Protect the local Electric Grid
(10)- How to EMP Protect Town Street and Traffic Lighting
(11)- How to EMP Protect Vehicles and Test Certification

Meanwhile, a major televised program was announced to all active stations in USA. It was being nationally tele- vised, plus webinars

and teleconferencing over central and Western USA. These presentations are extremely important as Nitanyahu of Israel delivered a few HPM (high power microwave) "miniature versions of the EMP" via drone to Iran putting them on notice that Israel will follow with an entire EMP event if Iran does not permit immediate UN inspection of designated facilities within the next two weeks.

Parenthetically, while North Korea has made overtures of sending one or more ICBMs with nuclear warheads headed for western USA, they fully understand that a single retalitory EMP event over North Korea will throw them back into the dark ages of 1870s. However, the fear and watchful alerts remains as a trigger may happen from one or more irrational sources. Thus, the world remains on edge and many speak of the coming of the long promised Armageddon. We shall see......

7.3 Cantdo-Bestville, Lessons Learned, Year 1

Needless to say there are many lessons learned here. These will be presented with the first ten major lesson now:

"Within a few months after an EMP attack, or any other event that causes long-term loss of the electric power grid, most people will become weary and despondent because of the hardship and starvation, and they will become desperate to get their modern civilization back. Without prior planning and action, this will take years.

Do you want to learn how to take steps to ensure that you can get modern civilization back quickly, or never lose it in the first place? Then, read or re-read the other half of this book on Bestville and see how they did it. This book and the many other expected outgrowth articles and other books will ensure that Cantvlle tragedies will never happen even if or when an EMP event does happen.

The Ten Most Important Lessons Learned on EMP Apathy and Protection

(1) **Become fully aware** of EMP = Electromagnetic Pulse, what it is, what damage it can do you, your family and your community. Recognize that it is real and going to happen – sooner or later, and that it is very subtle, does not kill people immediately, but starves and poisons people and produces a worst lifestyle unless prepared.

(2) **Be Prepared** – the boy scout motto. Get spun-up-to-speed. There are many articles and websites and a few books on the Internet. Be careful, for some are written by "Gloom and Doomers, especially re Solar Flares which may be the cause of electric power outage.

Here is where the fed. state or county government should issue an official guide to survival options with some template solutions, instead of abdicating their fiduciary responsibilities. So far, Hollywood has exacerbated the myths, and the EMP survivalists have grabbed the "low-hanging fruit", low lifestyle end by default. In time, TV educational materials and seminars will come to the rescue.

Speak to your senator, congress representative and local county supervisor to initiate action. Perhaps one or more local seminars can be started.

(3) **Government:** If the federal and states seem to be passive in supporting EMP awareness, preparation, training and education, consider executing this at the county level, for all 3,140 USA counties (average county size is 100,000 people). Make a consortium of the County Economic Development Office, the Chamber of Commerce, and a few lead officials from industry (architects/ engineers, banks, real estate and lawyers) and a few other county officials. Emphasis is citizen awareness, preparation, education and training.

Develop an on-going, periodically updated, booklet that consolidates the best of all county education materials, slide-shows, seminars, webinars and the like. This is done in four classifications as outlined in Chapter 2 of *EMP – Protect Family, Homes and Communities.* Therein the classifications are at a minimum: (1) Upper Quartile (top 25%), per Household Income, (2) Median per Household Income, (3), Lower Quartile, per Household Income, and (4) EMP Survivalists. There may be another or an additional split to reflect the differences in coastal vs. inland US locations, and Northern vs. Southern latitudes. Of course, any recipient may want to see the document for one or more other classifications to provide incentives for better locations or financial circumstances.

The Federal Government can help establish many empirical math models at their research labs, especially where there are so many variables. Many involve EMI and EMP simulated tests. For example:

(a) On the matter of grounding, the soil conductivity plays a major role. What measure of soil conductivity will account for a specified reduction of residual lead-in cable, common-mode current away from the building shield and drained to earth. Develop math models for architects, building designers and others to use.

(b) When attempting to shield the basement of an existing building, the footprint of the walls cannot be shielded since they cannot be accessed. Empirical models are needed to permit design considerations for other than new buildings. How much is shielding compromised?

(c) Data are needed on the susceptibility of vehicles and the ability to determine or forecast their dysfunctionality. Where are the microprocessor levels failing and at what levels. What kinds of retrofit kits might be offered to EMP harden them.

(d) What are the failure levels and how to EMP protect heart pacemaker,s hearing aids, electronic-control robotic body limbs, and other electronic implants. The present manufacturers have no idea and no provisions seem to exist for discovery.

(4) **Distribution Centers & Vehicles:** One of the biggest problems in surviving at the hamlet or village level and above is insufficient food, medications, and other timely replacement items from both inside and outside the EMP impacted area.

From inside the impacted village, there needs to be one or more warehouses that carry the more popular nutrients and things that negligent or forgetful families do not store. Where to draw the line is dependent on many variables, but a lot easier for the upper decile (10%) of wealthy counties.

From outside the impacted village, the best starting place is perhaps a satellite communications relay system so that designated inside locations can talk to outside providers. This implies that heavier use of the railroad and landing strip can be used as vehicles are too slow, consume too much fuel and are inefficient and inadequate of volume for long range replenishment deliveries.

(5) Recognize that the **EMP survivalist** are active on the Internet due to defaults in #(2) and (3) above. But, in going with long shelf-life food, water, medications, ammo and bartering items (money becomes almost worthless), they lose their jobs and lifestyle is worse only to that of no EMP preparation at all.

(6) **Water Distribution:** Perhaps, the most vital of all survivals is adequate drinking water plus water for other use. Gravity-drop reservoirs in non-flat lands are great. Else, one or more large water towers can be installed along with EMP protected, water pumps for tower water filling and solar panels for electricity supply. Here the water source should be nearby ponds, streams, rivers or reservoirs.

The use of swimming pools and other large non-drinking water containers can be readily converted to drinking water along the lines described in Chapter 3. Therein constructing a simple 25-50 gallon filtration system was described in detail. This can be done in advance for less than $200.

(7) **Financing:** Most of the financing incentive for going EMP protected is paid for by issuing County bonds. The Bond sinking funds are primarily retired from electricity payments that were previously paid to the electric utility before it became dysfunctional following an EMP event. Thus, the government does not have to provide financing incentives such as

Who Pays and Where Does the Money Come From?

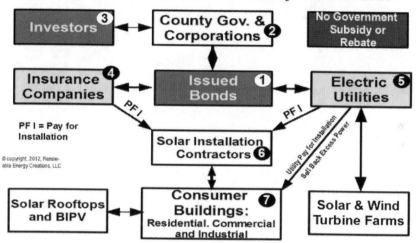

feed-in tariffs, rebates and tax credits for funding. Naturally, this is a big advantage vs. previous situations and enhances growth prospects.

(8) **Group Size:** The size of the EMP protection group or entity has a major impact on the survivability and the resulting lifestyle. The horizontal axis in the graph to the right is the group population size and the vertical axis is the resulting value judgment. The green line is the resulting lifestyle score. Note, the larger the group that is EMP protected, the higher is

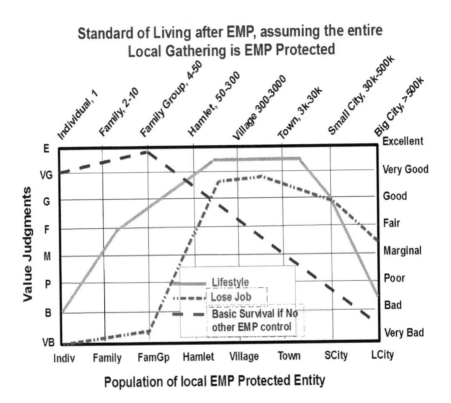

Standard of Living after EMP, assuming the entire Local Gathering is EMP Protected

the likely lifestyle scores until cities that have buildings above about four floors. This results since the solar rooftop cannot provide enough replacement for lost utility power. Crime then increases as the "Have Nots" break into other homes, stores and shopping malls.

(9) **Newbies:** Recognize that there also exist another big benefit beyond improved lifestyle in going EMP protection for larger group sizes. This app generates new (or modified)

EMP-protected products and services, opens up corresponding new markets which generate millions of jobs within a decade. If done at a large enough level, this will help pay down the $14 trillion national debt more than any other exercise. And, it is not mutually exclusive.

(10) **Entire Country; not just Civil Sector Involved**: It is understood that the USA Navy, portions of other USA military services, munitions and fuel storage, and selected Intelligence buildings and portions of the White House and Pentagon are already EMP protected with backup power.. To a large extent, this infrastructure represents locations where people work. However, more than 90% of the working population put on or take off their workplace hats and join the civil world on the way to and from work. They spend these remaining hours in transit, at home, shopping, sports, etc.. So, in reality, the entire nation needs to be EMP protected, not just some workplaces to ensure survival and at a level far beyond the bare minimum survivalists necessities.

The estimated cost of the above EMP protection over a 10-year period is well over $10 trillion, much of which is self financing. Remember self financing means (1) from electric bills otherwise or previously paid the electric utility, (2) revenues from taxes on the millions of newly employed, and (3) additional turnover from the money they spend to generate still more jobs and revenues. That is what capitalism and value added are all about. So, the concept of the entire EMP protection needs to be addressed by the government and industry planners. This is called EMP Protection Optimization illustrated below, and described elsewhere, some of which is seen on www.emp-safeguard.com.

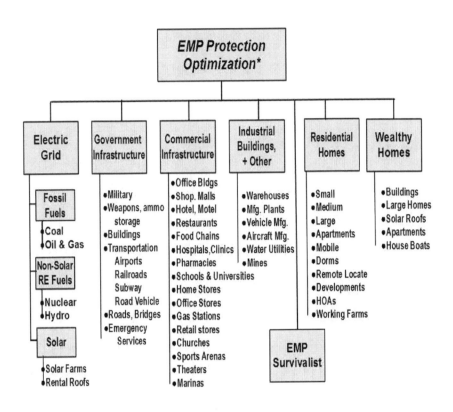

EMP Protection Optimization*

Electric Grid
- Fossil Fuels
  - Coal
  - Oil & Gas
- Non-Solar RE Fuels
  - Nuclear
  - Hydro
- Solar
  - Solar Farms
  - Rental Roofs

Government Infrastructure
- Military
- Weapons, ammo storage
- Buildings
- Transportation
  Airports
  Railroads
  Subway
  Road Vehicle
- Roads, Bridges
- Emergency Services

Commercial Infrastructure
- Office Bldgs
- Shop. Malls
- Hotel, Motel
- Restaurants
- Food Chains
- Hospitals, Clinics
- Pharmacies
- Schools & Universities
- Home Stores
- Office Stores
- Gas Stations
- Retail stores
- Churches
- Sports Arenas
- Theaters
- Marinas

Industrial Buildings, + Other
- Warehouses
- Mfg. Plants
- Vehicle Mfg.
- Aircraft Mfg.
- Water Utilities
- Mines

EMP Survivalist

Residential Homes
- Small
- Medium
- Large
- Apartments
- Mobile
- Dorms
- Remote Locate
- Developments
- HOAs
- Working Farms

Wealthy Homes
- Buildings
- Large Homes
- Solar Roofs
- Apartments
- House Boats

90

Part 2 of this Novel

*Read this novel for Separate
Reporting of Cantdo & Bestville.*

*For those who prefer to read
the sequential events of the
EMP unprotected town,
Cantdo, from day of EMP Burst
to one year later*

and, then,

*who may wish to read
the sequential events of the
EMP protected town,
Bestville, from day of EMP Burst
to one year later*

*This Part 2 reading is recommended
for those who wish a
more suspenseful and
exciting experience
via a novel*

Cantdo, Virginia

The EMP unprotected town

This section allows the reader to read uninterruptedly about Cantdo, from the day of the EMP event till one year later

Chapter 1, Cantdo, VA, Burst Day

Spring, at 3:00 p.m. (Unprotected Town.
Day of the EMP Burst)

Harris High School was letting out at 3:00 p.m. when students exiting the building noticed strangely that some cars and school buses were frozen-like in their different street positions. A few vehicle owners were seen gathered around their opened car hoods trying to determine what had just happened and the cause. One was seen running down the street seeking help.

A student ran back into the building to alert others of a strange street situation. Others outside started to call home on their cell phones and ipads. But, all mobile phone units were seen to be dysfunctional. Nothing appeared to work, whereupon frustration and confusion set in.

Meanwhile, the student who ran back into the building noticed others gathered around the assistant principal's office. One was trying to resuscitate him as he appeared to have expired – no breathing, or pulse. At that moment the principal reappeared to announce that Mr. Hopkins had a heart pacemaker which may have gone bad. But how? The secretary said she tried to call 9-11, but the phone had no dial tone. More confusion and disbelief set in on the gathering group.

Additional students exiting the building were quickly informed by the early birds of the weird disarray of vehicles and dysfunctional cell phones and ipads. While those having bikes quickly departed for home, others began to speculate at the curb about just what is happening. Then, one student said this looks like a scene from a book his dad was reading, called "One Second After". He said his dad remarked that a high altitude nuclear weapon burst would wipe out the electric grid and burn out nearly all electronics for hundreds of miles, maybe up to a thousand, while humans would not feel a thing on the ground. "Oh, my God", replied another. "Is this happening to us?" He added, "Maybe more are to follow and the next may be more destructive." Then, the group discussion became somewhat hysterical as more disbelief, fear and anxiety developed.

Most students had to walk home and noticed similar dysfunctional vehicles on the way. Many homeowners were seen in front of their homes and out in the street talking about the perplexing situation. Later upon arriving home, the two Harris High brothers, Hank and Jerry Drinkwell, also confirmed that the electricity was out and houses were dark. Also, their mother reported that the radio and TV were dead as well, and the house phones were not working.

Neighbors gathered in small groups speculating on what happened and what to do next. One observed that his old 1980 Pontiac hardtop was still working. Another said he had no water after flushing the toilet more than once. A third remarked that he had about 11,000 gallons of water in his home pool. He asked for opinions on how his water may become drinkable. The group speculated about the incongruity of events: No obvious terrorist attack as people, infrastructure and buildings are not destroyed. Yet, the electricity is gone. But, why no functional cells, radio and TV especially since some devices are battery operated?

Ken Atwater, a Pontiac car owner, returned to the group discussion. He had turned on his car radio and all he could get was static across the AM and FM bands. There were no stations from other Virginia cities or elsewhere? So one remarked, "What do we do now? We can't call the power company or emergency services; there appears to be no functional phones or vehicles?"

Jerry Drinkwell replied, "Oh my gosh! The frozen food in the fridge will go bad and we may run out of food, water and medication for grandma." Hank, Jerry's brother, remarked, "Help! Let's bike now over to Cantdo Shopping Mall and investigate. While it is nearing dusk, we have lights on our bikes, but maybe they won't work; there's almost no traffic, and maybe we can pick up some canned goods in the food center while there".

Chapter 2, One Day Later

Cantdo, VA (EMP Unprotected Town), Day 1

Word spread from mouth to mouth that the mayor, Mark Swanson, was to speak at 10:00 a.m. at the town plaza gazebo on the first day after the disaster event. Many of the population walked or arrived by bicycle and realized by then that there were no working computers, no Skype no teleconferencing; no radio; no TV nor any other way of communicating since it was quickly understood by most people that all electronics were indeed not functioning in addition to no electric utility power and no running water.

At 10:05 the meeting began, Mayor Swanson announced for all to come up close to the podium, bringing your bicycles as he had no public address system nor any other way to speak except at nearly a shouting level. He said his battery megaphone and backup generator were not working. His remarks then turned to a prayer to God to bless Cantdo and our entire nation as the mayor yet had no idea as to the expanse of their disaster exposure. He then introduced three people who would speak: the local hospital co-diretor, the chief of police, and a utility engineer who would first explain what is believed to have happened.

The electric power engineer, Chris Blue, said he is in charge of the 5th and Monroe street substation from which most of the town gets its electric power from the power plant. It then distributes the power around Cantdo via their overhead and buried local power lines.

He said, "To those of you who understand the phenomena, we have had an EMP, or nuclear Electromagnetic Pulse explosion – not a Solar Flare, such as a Geomagnetic Storm. The latter would represent at most a possible loss of the electric grid power. However, since the loss also contains no working radio, TV, phones and the like, only an upper atmosphere EMP explosion can do that since humans also do not feel a thing (Ed. caveat: those with heart pacemakers and hearing aids may have their devices burned out) and all infrastructure remains in tact. We are trying to learn what all this means and portends as we have not paid much attention to some of the earlier EMP warnings. I will report more tomorrow after I do more discovery."

"Meanwhile, we are not able to communicate with other villages, towns, or cities since we have lost all telecommunications. One car radio was found to pick up some long distance AM broadcast last night from locations believed to be over about 500 miles away."

Engineer Blue continued, "With few exceptions, we cannot drive anywhere or expect to receive out-of-town visitors since their vehicles are probably less than 20 years old and inclined to be more EMP susceptible due to their micro-processors. Our one long railroad siding and small 4,000 ft. air strip have had no traffic to inform us of what is going on outside of Cantdo. With that, I will turn you back over to Mayor Swanson."

Meanwhile, revisit the home of the Harris High School brothers, Hank and Jerry Drinkwell, at 10:00 a.m. Since school is closed, they just returned from a second store visit

97

by bicycle; this one to Well-Mart. The huge store was partly opened, but no lights except skylights and some fueled lanterns as the generators and microprocessor controls were all presumed to be burned out. Also, The refrigerated foods and beverage cases were still a little cool and people were taking out remaining contents, because there were posted, hand-written signs inviting them to do so, for free.

However, over in the canned goods section things were very different and somewhat ugly. The shelves were nearly empty and a few simultaneous arguments could be seen as people fought over who arrived there first. In one aisle, where there was only French bread and a few dozen other loaves left, a nasty fist fight erupted there. A few citizens tried to break up the battle and cool down emotions.

Cash registers were not working. Customers had to pay cash (no credit cards) and all items purchased had to be added up by hand by the cashier. Lines were very slow moving with very long waits. Shoe boxes were used as money containers.

The Well-Mart pharmaceutical section was in total disarray as some people had already ransacked the inside presumably in search of specific medications. It develops that the store manager had made the difficult decision to open the store to the food center and pharmaceuticals only with all other sections cordoned off. With no police or vehicles moving, and the canned goods shelves empty, the manager later decided to secure the entire building from further entry using only a handful of available employees.

Hank and Jerry's uncle, Don Follow, an assistant physician, arrived at their house after the Well-Mart trip to announce Cantdo's only hospital has about four days supply of fuel to run two surviving old non-electronic controlled generators;

the others were already dysfunctional. Thus, hospital hallways and most room lights are dimmed or out. Air conditioning was not working at all as their electronic controllers were also dysfunctional. Besides, they did not have enough generator fuel or power capacity to run them 24/7 anyway. Some COPD patients who require oxygen could no longer have this as the oxygen machine controllers are dead. While placed on tank oxygen, this would last for only two days at most. Refrigerated medications were only good for a few days as well. What then to do with all the hospital patients and employees, and lack of operational machines and devices?

The Drinkwell brothers and Uncle Don, also reported that two Cantdo citizens have died from unknown causes. The local undertaker could not get involved as his entire facility was without electricity and electronics. Funeral and burial services were unavailable for similar reasons. Also, no functional vehicles like a hearse for transport or backhoe for trench digging were available. In fact, the entire town of Cantdo, that offers services of all types, was shut down.

Chapter 3, Two Days Later

Cantdo, VA (EMP Unprotected Town), Day 2

The few older running cars drained empty the underground gasoline tanks of Timothy, the nearby Shell station as it was the only known station in Cantdo without a disabled pump. Timothy had kept it as a landmark antique with active pump to remind many of the locals of yesteryear's nostalgia. All other Cantdo gas stations were presumed dysfunctional including others at Timothy's as well. However, later some used hand pumps.

More than 90% of the Cantdo employees were not at work as their buildings had no power and all electronic controls were known or presumed to be burned out. This included lights, the telephone systems, computers, printers, building temperature controllers, elevators, security alarms, water heaters, toilets, and so on. Thus, folks are at home helping to focus more on family and friends survival.

Hank, Jerry, their sister and parents frequently met during the day to discuss resources and their conservation plans. This included, how to gain replenishments since all normal sources, such as regional distribution centers, are no longer available, nor are there any functional replenishment delivery trucks.

Their discussions lead to the Anderson family, and a few others of their local ilk, who are known to have practiced EMP survival preparation. They have stocked freeze-dried food with shelf lives of 10-25 years and other survival goods. Jerry remarked that the Anderson family may be under serious siege by looters seeking food, etc. As it developed, the Andersons may be ready to shoot any would-be burglars expected from the numerous new "Have Nots."

That afternoon, Hank and Jerry met with neighbors on both sides of their home. In comparing notes, one neighbor said his fridge is being used as an ice box and all remaining ice is about gone. They shared unfrozen food as it would soon become spoiled. Some of the meat was cooked using charcoal or wood on their outdoor, non-electric cookers.

Bottle water was a few days more in supply. However, the guy with the 11,000 gallon pool offered the neighbors to take bucket fulls and fill their bathtubs, toilets and other containers. Keep drinking water in the sinks. Then Jerry's Uncle Don from the hospital added that he knows of a way that pool water can be converted into into drinking water. This would be a good project for a few men to accomplish over several hours. However, this supposes we can get access to a small working generator (less than 5 kW) although there are other solutions. Here is how Don explained how it is done:

Get a plastic barrel, (wood will work if it doesn't leak) of at least 30 gallons. Get a hacksaw and a serrated edge knife.

(1) Cut the top off a plastic barrel with a knife and a hacksaw. Drill a half-inch drainage hole in the center of the bottom of the barrel.

(2- Line the bottom of the barrel with a cotton sheet.

(3)- Set the barrel on a stand. Use whatever works for the stand, such as sawhorses, cinder blocks or an old pallet, but remember you need to place the water storage container(s) beneath it.

(4)- Shovel sand into the barrel, filling the bottom of the barrel with an even 2- inch thick layer.

(5)- Shovel charcoal into the barrel until you create a 4-inch layer. Periodically smash the charcoal with the shovel. Breaking up any large chunks and ensuring there is a compact layer.

(6)- Fill the barrel with alternating layers of sand and charcoal, repeating steps 3 and 4 until the barrel is filled about 25% from the bottom. Make the last layer sand, even if it means making the charcoal layer beneath it thinner. This creates a reservoir for pouring pool water into it to the filter.

(7)- Place one hose from the drainage pump into the pool, and the other hose into the reservoir at the top of the barrel filter. Put the first storage container underneath the stand . Turn the generator pump on.

(8)- Adjust the speed of the pump so it roughly matches the speed at which the filter processes the water. When the purified water container is full replace it with the next one. It would be helpful if cleaned, used 1-gallon plastic bottles are used as they weigh only 8 pounds when full.

When no generator or power is available and there is a slope down from the swimming pool, a gravity-fed approach can be used via siphoning action

----

Don Follow went on to say that we need to spread this word over all of Cantdo, or the larger developments, or at least in those areas where homeowners have a pool or even a smaller jacuzzi or hot tub.

As more neighbors gathered in the late afternoon conversation, one remarked that the Cantdo's single Dept of Agriculture guy told them there are about 80 head of cattle and 50 pigs in suburbia Cantdo. This is barely enough to feed Cantdo for about one week or 10 days at most, when rationed with other foods. Fortunately canned goods on all our shelves might extend this up to a month. But, then what?

This subject lead into the subject of Cantdo family "victory food gardens" as most everyone had during WWII. Even a small amount of land, like 8' x 12' = 25 sq. ft. per person for a family of four, can grow several varieties of vegetables. Check the hardware and other stores (which may be closed) for seeds. While you are at it, get the old home canning book from the library (also probably closed) and pick up some jars and gaskets from the hardware store (probably closed, too) to can some food to carry many over the winter months. These may be hard to find.

The neighborhood gathering were reminded again of the above fortunate Anderson family and others like them who are survivalists, but whose lives may now be in jeopardy from desperate neighbor thieves. "Shame on us for not having seeds on hand or not having read books on EMP Survival", said Tommy Morgan, a 13 year-old boy scout present in the discussion. "So now you know our motto, 'Be Prepared'".

Then, Jerry remarked, "Finally, what about others from outside our neighborhood breaking into our homes to steal food and water. How many of us have guns and what is the ammunition supply? We have a lot of thinking and homework to do. Regrettably, we never took serious the Nuclear EMP warnings and publications over the past few years."

Thus, belated or not, Jerrry said, "Let us form a local group, both to ensure we know who we can trust and to determine the strength of our group resources." All agreed and the new session began inpromptu.

Chapter 4, One Week Later

Cantdo, VA (EMP Unprotected Town), Week 1

Because several shots fired have been reported, some people are becoming desperate. Thus, Mayor Swanson formed a group of advisers, beyond the three that were introduced at the town gazebo meeting last week. They meet for about a half hour, daily, to report larger problem topics needing fixing, review the priorities, and make assignments. There would be five such groups: (1) food and drinking liquids, (2) medications, hospital and nursing-home, (3) fuel, vehicles and generators, (4) processing, location and burial of the dead, and (5) all other. Of course, with few exceptions, no one is any longer employed and all support is voluntary which makes the outcome and control nearly impossible or at least, very challenging..

The owner of Ames funeral home remarked that there were about 14 deaths last week, most coming from the hospital and nursing homes because of lack of oxygen and dialysis machine failures. The decedent cannot be embalmed or cremated as Ames and the two other funeral homes have no electric power. One suggestion has been made to move the decedent bodies out to the edge of the town trash dump, and make a common burial pit since the dirt is loose and the pit has to be dug by hand. (Remember no front loaders or backhoes are any longer functional).

Another employee of Ames remarked that they do not have a suitable vehicle that works. A third said there are a few horses in town and several flat wagons. Three volunteered to study the problem and return in two days with a best recommen-dation that can be implemented immediately. But, remember, this is hard to do since we have no working telephone, cell, computer or other communication.

Police chief, Mike Tolstoy reported that there have been three deaths from being shot due to home burglaries seeking food and water. Two more are dying from wounds, but there is no way to take them to the hospital, which can't help anyway because of other priority problems. For example, the hospital has no refrigeration and all such medications are being lost. Several of the staff is sleeping there due to exhaustion and lack of transportation. Their food supply is nearing depletion.

Bill Matovich, of the Fish and Wildlife Service, reported that the deer population is one source of food not estimated with the cows and pigs, now having been about 25% consumed. An ardent archer, Bill reports that he estimates there may be roughly 100 deer within 10 miles, and maybe many hundreds of rabbits. The game warden kicked in that fishing has already been increased tenfold. And perhaps 20 of the egrets, cranes and other bigger birds have been killed. Someone sarcastically joked, "Don't forget your pet dogs", which drew some nasty stares and snarls.

Bill Matovich then introduced Zig Campbell, a naturalists expert on wild edible plants. His masters thesis a few years ago was on how to help survive in the wilderness. Zig said, "It is important to get from the library, if it is still open or accessible, a plant identification book. Two examples are *A Field Guide to Edible Wild Plants*, by Lee Peterson, or the U.S. Army *Illustrated Guide to Edible Wild Plants*. Remember, do not eat bitter tasting plants and milky juice plants. They may be poisonous, and, avoid wild mushrooms as risks are high.

"Your list should contain many fruits: wild grapes, strawberries, mulberries, raspberries, blueberries, blackberries. elderberries, apples, (not in the wild: oranges, tangerines, and grapefruit).

"Collect nuts from hickory, walnut and acorn trees, but roast to destroy parasites.

Among the edible plants are dandelions; Queen ante's lace; pigwood. chicory and purslane leaves, chickweed and wild onions.

" Don't forget frogs and turtles. Over 1,000 insects are eaten worldwide by humans including beetles, bees, wasps, ants, grasshoppers, crickets, moths and butterflies." Matovich concluded, "There are many more. The foregoing barely scratches the surface. So, get one of the above books cited ASAP."

Meanwhile, back at Hank and Jerry's home, Jennie, the younger sister, reported to her dad, Tom Drinkwell, and brothers that we are all beginning to smell through lack of bathing or showering. She stated, "There is no running water and, of course, there is no hot water as all electricity is gone." She also complained, "We are out of toilet paper, and I am tired of scooping out and emptying our toilet from human waste and dumping it in a neighborhood empty lot. I have already stepped in someone else's waste".

Since nearly all Cantdo working inhabitants have lost their jobs following the EMP event, Jerry's father, Tom, suggested that the family is well overdue for a complete reassignment of duties. The banks in town are all closed, and besides cash is rapidly becoming worthless, they need to establish barter items to trade with others. And there must be some scheduling

106

of hunting expeditions. Finely, they must consolidate this with the immediate neighbors and a few others as they too have similar needs. Here is the starter list of what Tom Harris has come up with, subject to family discussion and re consolidation with the neighbors:

List for Family Jobs and Chores Assignments

Task Identification	Hank	Jerry	Jenny	Dad	Mom
Hunting in woods for food	X	X			
Pool water purification	X	X			
Rainwater harvesting				X	
Fishing at Timberland Pond	X	X	X		
Get wood & fuel for cooking	X				
Food preparation & cooking			X		X
Food Garden Preparation		X			
Food Garden Maintenance			X		
Water carrying for bathing		X			
Inside household chores			X		X
Clothes sewing & Washing					X
Inside house maintenance				X	
Outside house chores & maintenance				X	
Dig pits in yard for garbage & waste	X	X			
Neighbor meeting & consolidating				X	X
Daily 15 min family meeting	X	X	X	X	X
ID and tagging bartering items				X	
Help out at church				X	X
Task Identification	Hank	Jerry	Jenny	Dad	Mom

Tom Drinkwell suggested that in addition to the starter list, we take a one day break for each of us to review, to add to the list any item taking more than two hours a week, and to replace the "X" in the list cells with an estimate of the hours per week it will take to accomplish. Then we meet in two days to consolidate. Although the family is all cooperative the overhanging gloom was very apparent. And, yipes! This is only the first week..

Chapter 5, One Month Later

Cantdo, VA , (EMP Unprotected Town), Month 1

At their daily meeting, Mayor Swanson introduced Dr. Blemming, who summed up that our Cantdo town population was about 10,500. In a normal month we have about 15 deaths and 17 births. However, one month after EMP, we have over

Reaons for Death in USA, 2009 Records

Women Reason for Death	%	Men Reason for Death	%
Heart disease	24	Heart disease	25.2
Cancer	22.2	Cancer	24.4
Stroke	6.3	Injuries	6.2
Chronic Lower respirtory	5.9	Chronic Lower respiratory	5.3
Alzhalimer's disease	4.5	Stroke	4.3
Injuries	3.5	Diabetics	2.9
Diabetics	2.8	Suicide	2.4
All Else	31.8	All Else	29.3

200 deaths so far including some infants who couldn't make it to the hospital or clinic. No midwives nor helpers could be found. "The death population is mostly elderly sector from lack of medication and physicians care. In this respect, examine what people die from in normal times in USA as shown in placard table I now hold up for all to see," said Dr. Blemming.

Risk Rate vs. Blood Pressure

Blood Pressure	Risk Rate*
115-75	Normal
135-85	2X
155-95	4X
175-105	8X

*Applies as multiplier to the normal risk of Heart Attacks or Stroke
Novartis Pharmaceuticals

"Now, one month later, the Cantdo hospital and a few of the local clinics are almost closed for business. No electricity; no medication requiring refrigeration; no air conditioning; no lights, oxygen nor dialysis machines, etc. Without any functional MRIs, Cat Scanners, or X-Ray machines, and few attending physicians, nurses and other helpers, Cantdo population will now start dying in larger percentages. For example, about 30% of decedents normally die from heart attacks and strokes. When this is compared to a person with increasing blood pressure, his or her death rate increases exponentially. This is shown by my assistant holding up the second placard above", stated Dr. Blemming.

In his verbal report, police chief Mike Tolstoy said, "Those killed from home burglaries are strongly on the rise. A few remarked that they no longer have ammo and Spikes Gun Shop said they are almost out of the popular 9 mm and shotgun shells. They already had a shop break in and some hand guns were stolen in the first week."

"Arson seems to be on the rise as are suicides. Unfortunately, no fire trucks are working so that we just hope for the rains and less wind. Community shelters are also very heavily attended and soon will run out of supplies, not the least being food and water."

A neighborhood cook-out "feast" was to be planned before the hunters returned. Fortunately, there is still some hand butane igniters available to start the fires and most of the fuel is cut wood as nearly all the charcoal is gone. Cigarettes are no more and smokers have lost or misplaced most of their hand lighters.

The hunters, Hank and Jerry Drinkwell and their friend returned from hunting with two deer and three rabbits to their favor. One deer was skinned and disembowel at the party grounds while some others looked on. One of the fire pits, prepared for the party, was converted to process (cook) the deer. The party continued on with blessings for better times to come amongst all the gloom and doom. Just wait till the gathering is over and all return to the scary and uncertain future awaiting them. Some people are beginning to give up hope.

One couple joined the party late to announce that they bicycled over near Deep Creek development when a helicopter circled several times and then landed in an open field, near the gate house. Many of the residents ran to the chopper to find out what was happening. The pilot told them they are from Chesapeake Naval Base and are instructed to survey the areas and report back. When he told them he also had several medications and some food and water on board, a few nutty desperadoes in the group immediately rushed and overtook the pilot, knocking him to the ground. They fought over the boxes and two including the pilot were shot in the ensuing fight. Then a sad recognition set in as (1) no report was yet unfolded regarding the expanse of the EMP outage or (2) no one knew how to operate the helicopter to fly wherever.

The next day, Hank and Jerry critiqued the helicopter incident and realized that there is some active life at the military air and ship bases on coastal regions, especially on the Chesapeake and around Newport - Hampton - Norfolk, about 180 miles away from Cantdo. They also reasoned (guessed) that those neighboring areas may have been spared the EMP aftermath or at least with boats and ships can go afar to gain provisions. After all, an aircraft carrier sports 4,000 swabbies alone. So, why not go there and find out. But how?

Hank and Jerry also spent some time on pausing and reflecting on why they have not considered moving out of Cantdo long before now. There are some known villages that are believed to have partly become EMP protected and therefore enjoy some sembledge of lifestyles in contrast to Cantdo. The helicopter event served to remind them that it is time for serious reflection. Were it not for family and a few friends, and the extreme difficulty of travel, they would have been gone long before now.

Jerry said, "Ken Atwater, the 1980 Pontiac hardtop guy, must know of his other fortunate older car owners who we might convince to join us or borrow their vehicle for a consideration in sharing the outcome".

Jerry then added "With all the scores of cars stuck in various roads and streets, their gas tanks must still have quantities of fuel. Using Ken's Pontiac or our bicycles with a trailing small wagon we can go to Pep Boys, NAPA or Sears."

Hank interrupted, "We can break in if the store is not open and bring back at least twelve, 5-gallon plastic cans for storing 60 gallons of petrol. This would get us over 420 miles for a round trip to Norfolk and other areas." Hank concluded, "However, fuel alone would weigh 450 pounds and waste petrol with the load, so why not have six 5-gallon cans full and the rest empty for possible future filling elsewhere."

Conclusion: after arranging for borrowing an old car in fairly good repair and getting the gas cans, they will get a detailed map of Virginia and plan the trip carefully. Unfortunately with no computer, they cannot use map websites. Food, water, money, other provisions and time to plan the trip would be needed.

But, as it developed their father overheard their discussions and cut in with, " Hey, guys, why not bring your ideas to Mayor Swanson's office and discuss them. He could arrange to get the car, gas cans, plus a letter of introduction from his office that you can show any Marshall stopping you about your mission."

In fact, their dad went on to say "There are several logistic facts like extent of region with EMP aftermath, when help might arrive, etc. that we need to know here in Cantdo. What say you?"

They decided to go to bed and discuss it in the morning. But, Jerry and Hank weren't convinced about "when help will arrive and other wishful considerations."

In another meeting held locally the same day with about fourty concerned Cantdo citizens at the local closed college library, erstwhile real estate broker, Harold Swanson, was preparing for a long awaited presentation regarding Project Zebra.

Swanson began "I welcome you folks to this long awaited meeting resulting from many requests to me from you as individuals. This to let you know in advance that most of what I have to say is not good news but does provide some hope and expectations if certain measures can be taken after a most catostrophic EMP incident last month."

Swanson continued, "The Bronxville Evening News ran an article on April 23, 2013 Times Herald, *'An Almost Economic and Financial Market Loss.'* *'Today*, the stock market almost lost about $200 billion dollars for a few minutes on a Twitter-hacked rumor of a White House explosion, before correcting. This resulted from many software account trigger, sell-order programs having a loss mitigation, safety protection action."

Swanson added, "Suppose the rumor had been a sudden EMP burst instead, in which the electric grid went down along with all RAM and backup memory that became dysfunctional. Even flash memory was burnt out by being connected to a mother board. All the stock brokerage houses, banks, insurance companies, retirement funds, annuity records and the like back-up memory were lost. Are your equity records in the hands of others EMP non-protected institutions? Can you prove your loss to the institutions who have also become dysfunctional ? Are your life savings gone in a heartbeat?"

Swanson continued, "The above true story of the April 23, 2013 stock market event was self correcting because of software escape protections. Today, the real EMP event was a month ago and all retirement funds, savings accounts, annuities peculiar to the EMP impacted area will be lost in their records, a few exceptions notwithstanding. Social security records, however, are also housed in EMP unaffected areas, so records are not lost."

Harold Swanson added, "However, the problem gets even bigger. How are the monthly retirement funds, annuities, even social security checks going to be delivered (or electronic transfer) to Cantdo retirees when there is no mail delivery because of dysfunctional vehicles and no gas stations, extremely little communication, no Internet and so on. Thus, all your monthly subsistances are no longer possible and records may never be re-created."

Upon hearing this, mass bedlem broke out at the meeting with some of the audience fainting and screeming, cursing and the like. Two CPR attempts were initiated. The scene quickly got out of control and Harold Swanson immediately realized he had committed a catastrophic no-no by not having told individuals or families separately and in a far more couched manner. Too late now! How to overcome this?

Chapter 6, Three Months Later

Cantdo, VA , (EMP Unprotected Town), Month 3

As an update to the Drinkwell brothers plan to have an expedition to Newport News two months earlier, they did follow their dad's advice and engage Mayor Swanson's office. Therein, they received an affidavit for their travels and their mission "on behalf of Cantdo" seeking support from the Naval installations or others. Hank and Jerry also got their plastic gas cans and other materials and goods for the 210-mile trip.

A Naval helicopter landed at Cantdo bearing news and some provisions, plus Jerry Drinkwell. Regrettably, Hank, Jerry's brother had died from food poisoning and their vehicle was stolen. The helicopter pilot reported that the demands on the several Naval basis has turned out to dispersing food, water and goods to scores of towns and cities along most of the East Coast and several hundred miles inland. The pilot apologized for the infrequent visit from their Naval base, but their survival replenishment mission is severely overloaded.

The pilot did provide some encouragement that the Seaport at Charleston, SC has been receiving steam locomotives from Europe and Australia so that major railroads can distribute replenishments to the hundreds of towns and cities in Eastern USA. The Naval helicopter also contained 20 short-wave, battery-operated radios so Cantdo can keep in touch with the rest of USA and Canada and gain some expectations about survival relief. The radios also have hand-cranked generators to ensure power for being kept informed when the batteries were consumed.

Another major meeting took place at the town gazebo at 10:00 a.m. There Mayor Swanson and several of the close working groups reported the following:

Scores of premature deaths from water and food starvation and from food poisoning. It is estimated that about one third of the Cantdo population has died from several causes especially from salmonella breakouts and other epidemics. There are no undertaker or funeral services. Decedents are buried in three main areas: large open pits in nearby Saulton woods, the city dump, and at the cemetery.

Most horses, and all cattle and pigs were gone. Discussions did turn to killing pets for food. It is estimated that half the population have already killed their pets for food and to save feeding them as well. House burglaries are routine. Most other stores were not raided as word gets around that they have already had break-ins and been picked over.

Almost no contact with neighboring towns or elsewhere with almost no telecom and travel vehicles, no airplane, train or bus are operational.

There were some discussions about eating those of recent death with no disease. Ammunition for self protection was running low. Emergency services are no longer available.

Hope was all but gone as there was little expectations of any relief vehicles or prospects. Suicides and shootings were on the increase.

Meanwhile, back at the Drinkwell home, they were comparing progress on their Task Assignment list. Since, Hank had regrettably perished as reported before. The list has grown and there are fewer family members to help out.

Jenny reported that she has a gigantic tooth ache and there exists no dentists to help out especially since the dentist has no electricity. Having had an earlier root canal operation, the family was at loss what to do other than tooth extraction. Maybe Dr. Smallwood, the dentist, could be found to see if he has any novacain or can help out in some way, if he hasn't died too. However there is no operational vehicle nor any gasoline fuel available. Can't call him on cell or telephone since neither works. All very discouraging and demoralizing.

So Tom Drinkwell, Jenny's father, described what options exist for tooth removal default. First, they still have some Advil tablets in their pantry closet. Start by taking two. Remember they are not an anesthesia. Tooth extraction is not an enjoyable experience as it is, and will be less so in a long-term survival situation with no power and limited supplies as we have here. Unlike baby teeth, a permanent tooth is unlikely to be removed simply by wiggling it out with your (gloved) hand or tying a string to it and the nearest doorknob and slamming the door. Also, be aware that pieces of jaw bone that are very firmly attached to the root of the tooth can sometimes come out during the extraction. Tom and Jerry will immediately try to locate a doctor or dentist who can help out

----

In a more positive vein, two of the mayor's group leaders reported:

(A)- The vegetable garden started almost three months ago

was a major success and had high priorities for survival, but produce was too early to harvest, which would start in a few weeks.

About 30 families moved out to Cantdo's suburbia where 14 farms are located. They were housed and slept in barns and other farm shelters. They helped the farmers in expanding the vegetable farming, and restarting cattle and pig farming from the mated pairs delivered by the helicopter pilot. Fuel was obtained from EMP disabled abandoned vehicles as mentioned earlier. While the newer tractor microprocessor's were burned out, the older tractors still worked. Enough to till the fields (and the older backhoes were used to dig burial pits for the deceased)

(B)- The earlier discussion on how to develop drinking water from swimming pools was a major reason for otherwise fewer deaths. There were a few hundred pools located in Cantdo that carried out the process discussed in an earlier chapter. While cooking and filter charcoal had run short, they learned how to make charcoal from selected woods – sometimes an arduous undertaking. This is done in the following manner:

Materials needed: A propane heater (usually available at hardware stores for $35) with propane gas tank, a charcoal chimney (stove pipe 4-12" in diameter) and with internal can (one to 5-gallon paint can) somewhat smaller in diameter containing three holes punched in the top, and channel locks for removing the hot can containing the wood pieces to be converted to charcoal) . A supply of wood with preferences for pine or willow.

(1)- Place the charcoal chimney on top of the burner and connect the burner to the propane gas supply.

(2)- fill the empty paint can with several pieces of broken up wood with larger pieces around the outside wall. Put the lid with holes back on the paint can and place inside the chimney.

(3)- Ignite the burner (hand igniter or cigarette lighter) and cook

for about 1-1/2 hours. Cook at a low-medium level – not too fast or it won't work.

(4)- When white smoke comes out the three holes that is a sign of dry distillation in which steam and resin in the wood are being cooked.

(5)-When the steam turns to a grayish-brown color, shortly thereafter, flames will come out the three holes in the paint can – a sign that the process is nearly over. The oils are burned off.

(6)- Remove the inner paint can with the tongs and turn it upside down on th dirt ground to block oxygen from getting therein. Leave to cool down.

(7)- Break up the charcoal wood into small pieces. Place the contents into a larger container for later use.

(8) Note: There are other somewhat similar ways to make larger quantities of charcoal not discussed here.

Chapter 7, One Year After

Cantdo, VA (EMP Unprotected Town), Year 1

Arrangements were set for a gathering in memory of the first anniversary of the EMP event. About 1,000 of the town's population remain or 10% of the original 10,500 population, have survived. The survivors are mostly the young and healthy who have also developed an enormous street smarts by learning, pragmatically, what works and what does not. Unfortunately, without the Internet and other sources on survival, the population was ill equipped to deal with a major disaster, let alone an EMP event. How sad, in retrospect, that Cantdo took the entire EMP warnings for years as though nothing like this would ever happen.

The death rate would have been much greater were it not for the many developed food gardens, both large and small, and both inside Cantdo and its outskirts. Thanks to the railroad siding, nearly all external replenishments (but far-far under needs) arrived by rail later via wood-burning steam engines. The 4,000-foot dirt landing strip was never installed as in EMP-protcted towns. However, much of the survival credit goes to the small body of family EMP survivalists who were well equipped but constantly harassed by the Have Nots.

In retrospect, one sad thing about Cantdo, is that the concept of "Vital Replenishments" was never addressed (other than locally) when it had opportunities to reflect upon earlier consideration of some degree of EMP protection. No dirt runway was chosen as planners assumed there was no communications with survival. Yet, the unsuspected earlier helicopter arrival at Cantdo brought a 500 watt transmitter with solar panel to let the rest of the country know about its status. With this and the several protected short-wave radios, a closed loop of communications is possible re deliverance of vitals (freeze-dried fool, popular medications, hunting shotgun ammo) by a Globemaster discussed in sections 6.2 and 6,3 in this faction book.

So with all the above food gardens and plantings, food was no longer very scarce, but then remember, 90% of the population of Cantdo had also perished. Canning could not be done as few knew how to do it and there were no canning jars or jar gaskets to be found. Meat was no more except for occasional squirrel, rabbit, possum or raccoon. All else had been over hunted in the surrounding areas by Cantdo hunt parties who often brought back no catch. Similarly birds and fish were few and far between.

The death rate from starvation and disease were dominant. Many more were from hepatitis, injuries and some amputations at the residue of the hospital, ill-equipped to handle more than becoming a morgue. However, the two older generators, had finally been retired as there was no more fuel. More than a thousand gallons of gasoline had been siphoned from stalled vehicles within ten miles. The fuel was put into container cans and brought to the hospital for generator use for limited lighting, surgery, and other critical medical uses.

Bestville, Virginia

The EMP protected town

This section allows the reader to read uninterruptably about Bestville , from the day of the EMP event till one year later

Chapter 1, Bestville, VA, Burst Day

Spring, at 3:00 p.m. (Protected Town.
Day of the EMP Burst)

Because of sudden EMP electric power outage warnings from transfer alarms and sirens used at 3:02 p.m., Bestville, the EMP protected town, folks were informed that unless already in use, their backup power is activated. Unknown to most, whether at home, work, shopping mall, or elsewhere, their solar rooftop and back-up batteries are operational (already) or taken over from the electric utility power loss.

Nearly all car and truck vehicles were operational, and most cell phones, ipads and laptops and e-book readers were working, but only for local communication within their Bestville township. Distant located source radio and TV broadcast, telephone and cell service were non functional. Satellite communications to distant non-EMP event locations and fiber-optic links continued to work. The one local radio station was functional with news of the emergency announcements. The principal reasons being that their buildings are all EMP protected and each has its own protected solar rooftop, battery bank and generator.

Later, it was surprisingly discovered that nearly all electrical and electronics were dysfunctional in one food market. This means no cash register or air conditioning was working. Also, there was no lights, no public address, etc. Explanations for this apparent anomaly, were that the store failed to construct a double door and vestibule entry to prevent EMP leakage if the event happened at the very moment of a person entering or exiting the building as shown in the illustration.

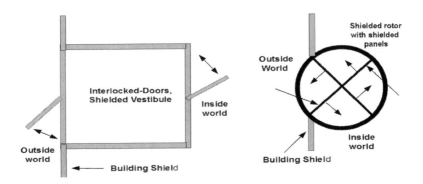

Following redundant confirmation at 3:12 p.m. of the EMP event: (1) the town sirens gave alert notice as did (2) the launching of several loud-speaker vehicles traveling the streets of Bestville. further, the above announced radio station reminded all listeners that the inevitable EMP event, regrettably, has just happened. This means the following actions and recommendations apply as stated in the prologue of your EMP warning and preparation books. A surprisingly well controlled response by the listeners, demonstrated the value of the many weeks and months of indoctrination and training. In other words, Bestville, so far, seemed to have practiced the Boy-Scouts' motto, "Be prepared." But wait! We have only just started....

One elevator was stuck in the hospital between floors. A later maintenance check showed that the electronic elevator controls, are located inside of a shack on the roof. Apparently, the bonding of the shack to the rooftop screen was not properly done by the installer. Of more concern, inside that shack on the EMP test confirmation clipboard form, the installation EMP shielding test was either never done or not recorded, a clear lack of quality control. Perhaps, this was a victim of the lack of wide experience in building shielding.

By the way, Audiobond Hearing Co., received a few phone calls that their clients, who were outdoors when the EMP event took place, reported that their hearing aids stopped working. Later it was determined that nearly all medical devices have never been tested to meet EMP exposure levels, other than another maximum spec at 100 V/m of RS-105. What does the FDA have to say about this?

On the positive side, the town Mayer, Pete Henderson, his staff and Barr EMC Corporation received a lot of credit for the remarkable EMP protection that their company and others have done to make Bestville relatively EMP immune.

Chapter 2, One Day Later

Bestville, VA (EMP Protected Town), Day 1

Many of the Bestville residents were tuned in on their one local radio station to learn the extent of what has happened in their own town and other locations within USA . They were able to do this as their radios were functional because their buildings were EMP protected and the Radio station was protected as well. Someone remarked that their external antennas had protective band-pass filters inserted to receive the broadcast inside of their shielded buildings, but otherwise had blocked the EMP from entry.

Mayor Henderson was making a number of announcements at 9:30 a.m. Others in his group would speak about what was happening. After a brief introduction, the electric utility substation engineer; Ted Barron, reported that their satellite communication relay system, that connects to Richmond, the state capital and Washington, DC (special EMP protected also), disclosed the following.

We have had a presumed terrorist attack by an unidentified source(s) that launched three simultaneous EMP weapons over USA. For the West Coast and Central USA, enemy missiles were intercepted and destroyed by our military anti-missile missiles. However, the terrorist missile from a container ship detonated on the East Coast got through and exploded taking down electric power and destroying most electronics from South Carolina to Massachusetts on the North (800 miles), and from the Atlantic Ocean to Easten

Ohio on the West (600 miles). Except for a few other EMP protected towns and some military base locations, Naval Ships, Intelligence buildings and selected other infrastructure, Bestville is the only central East Coast protected town. This radio station will keep you informed throughout the day with all updates.

The mayor then introduced the Chief of Police, Harold Shultz, and the director of the county Economic Development Office. Schultz said all listeners should review pages 11 through 14 of their EMP Emergency Planning Guide to refresh what to do and not to do regarding contacting family and friends and others in the EMP impacted areas. Remember, you can't communicate since their phones, cells, ipads and other communication units are almost certainly burned out. However, some satellite communications links may still be open.

Do not attempt to drive to any locations affected because (1) you will not be able to get gas or diesel fuel along the way, or especially (2) you may be stopped and your vehicle may be high jacked by desperate people. Also, the area may be under Marshall law and the national guard may stop you and force you to return to Bestville. Focus your energies on self survival of our Bestville town, at least for the present.

Mayor Henderson reminded all listeners and other Bestville residents that they were given a daily diary book to write down their experiences. These include, those relative to what equipment and the working condition of the electronics they own, dates and time. The option to do this using their computers is a practical alternative. These data will later be of great value to other county economic development offices, state governments and the Feds when they update their master EMP protection analysis and planning directory.

Meanwhile, back at the local Well-Mart, the town radio reporter and his photographer were documenting the activities. Some of the overhead electric lights were turned off as well as most of the A/C in the non-food center and pharmaceuticals areas to conserve generator fuel, although their solar rooftop can handle most of the electrical load during non overcast daytime.

Canned food goods were fairly picked over since there is no food distribution center in Bestville. The closest is Stoberton, 60 miles away and they are not known to survive the unprotected areas. However it was rumored that some replacement supplies may be arriving in about five days by our own wood-burning steam engine freight train and lesser quantities by air at our small local airfield. However, the uncertainties always causes people to hoard supplies for fear of the unknown in spite of all the indoctrination and preparation earlier on.

In summary, Mayer Henderson said, "Thank God and all those involved in the preparation work that went into making Bestville an EMP protected town. It is especially gratifying that very few folks lost their jobs such as those who receive and give directions to those outside of our township. However, remember, that for most of those receiving retirement and social service checks, this may be indefinitely discontinued. Thus our Plan, Zebra, discussed in the next chapter, goes into effect immediately for them.

Chapter 3, Two Days Later

Bestville, VA, *(EMP Protected Town)* Day 2

The radio announcements in Bestville spoke of a number of quick seminars some volunteers agreed to present over the coming week. The first involves the subject of telecommunications covering several priority aspects as they are vital to our ultimate survival and to permit us to optimize what we do over the forthcoming weeks and months – maybe even years. There will be time reserved for questions and answers during the seminars.

The first short one hour course given by Zack Thompson, a professor at the Bestville college, indicated a number of things we need to know on a regular basis. While some of these are in our indoctrination manuel that all residents have, they need to be given significant visibility now:

(1)- Our groceries, water, medications and fuel for our vehicles will run low unless certain planned replenishment actions come to pass in a timely manner. For example, since we have the map of the entire East Coast area that is dysfunctional, except for our Bestville and four other protected areas,, we need to identify the nearest cities of, say, 50,000 people or more on the periphery of the area having electricity and communications. This is achievable only via our satellite relay communications. Remember, these contacts are needed since one or more of these sources will become hubs for railroad and/or aircraft arriving here on a predetermined bases, as mentioned, with replenishments of food, medications and other provisions.

(2)- While our cell phones, ipads and the like work locally within our 75 sq. mile Bestville area, we need to devise a satellite or fiber optic link to central and west coast functional areas. Once we have that link we can make contact with many provision suppliers. But remember, nearly 100,000,000 Americans in the dysfunctional East Coast areas will be making very competitive demand for similar supplies. However they lack the communication means.

(3)- Although metro Washington, DC is in the same dysfunctional area, much of the pentagon, intelligence agencies and other Government Departments are EMP protected, but their nearby homes are not. So we need to make telecom contact there to ensure we get priority over other sectors vying for the same needs. This could become a logistical nightmare.

(4) Remember that Norfolk and Newport News are a home to a large sector of the US Navy fleet at any time. Since they are EMP protected, so will be their secured food, water and medication storage in adjoining areas. Thus, we must resume earlier established communications with contacts there.

(5) Now, listen carefully as this is the most important announcement reminder. We will have time for Q&A throughout the following discussions.

While it was hoped that many other neighboring villages, towns and cities would have had EMP protection by now, that is not the case. Since they know of our EMP protected town, we can expect some unfriendly visits. Therefore, we now pass out an orange band you are to wear immediately and at all times, to distinguish between Bestville citizens and others

130

who may have entered here with unfriendly motives. Be Sure you don't tell others why you wear his band.

How can they enter? A few vehicles may still be functional. Or they may come by motor scooter, bicycle or in some cases by foot. The four main roads of entry and exit to Bestville will have an armed police officer assisted by one rotating volunteer to guard, question and interrogate visitors. This is not to imply that we will reject all visitors, though we will help them if we have more than sufficient supplies. This statement will be discussed later as we will have a few other volunteers watching other ways of entry.

The important matter of further discussion on project Zebra, on receiving pension funds and social security payments in a timely manner has not been forgotten. We will report on this with updates in the next two weeks.

Chapter 4, One Week Later

Bestville, VA (EMP Protected Town), Week 1

The one daily a.m. Bestville broadcast station is now operated from 6:00 a.m. till midnight to keep all residents informed on post-EMP activities, news, assignments, warnings, critique and the like. However, town "classified information" is excluded since the broadcast might be picked up by other areas who may have listeners with ill-motives in mind. Thus, the daily mayor's meeting is still to be held at town hall grounds at 9:00 a.m. The mayor's messengers spread the word around of this and to be sure to wear your orange Bestville citizen ID bands.

At the mayor's meeting, Police Chief, Harold Schultz announced that Bestville, a town of low crime, is even lower as most all residents are extending helpful hands to fellow neighbors at these uncertain times. Also, since Bestville has a 98% EMP protection of its resident's homes and their workplaces and store fronts, there is no reason for EMP-generated "Have Nots" and the crime that would follow. For the few exceptions the positive neighborly, share attitude comes to the rescue. The local farmers are especially noted for their offers to help out and share some of the farm crop harvesting.

Regrettably, there was almost a skirmish at dusk yesterday when one of our resident neighborhood watch guards intercepted two intruders not wearing the orange Bestville ID arm bands. At gunpoint, our guard asked them from where they came. They replied from Jeston, a village about 15 miles away. He gave them a few provisions and told them to return immediately or they may get shot if not placed in jail as our town is off limits to intruders. Be sure to spread the word that unwelcomed out-of-town intruders risk being shot.

However, it is observed if visitors must communicate with Bestville, stop by guardpost #1 on Route 360 South. We will not discourage friendly solicited help exchange, but we must take care of our own first. A few of our locals exhibited concern that we need a more refined approach to arriving visitors. For example, what does the guard say if the visitor needs access to a dialysis machine as his hospital is dysfunctional? Obviously, we need a brief manual explaining what to do since this kind of preparation unfortunately escaped our broad post-EM manual preparation guide coverage.

At the mayor's meeting, the town supervisor, Tony Costello, announced that only about two percent of the population lost their jobs since the EMP event. Those individuals working mostly at motels depend upon out-of-town activities for their employment, such as tourism and a product imports and exports.

Regarding Project Zebra, mentioned earlier, the elderly inquired about their monthly social security and some asked about mail and parcel delivery. Regional Banker, Harold Johnson, replied that some local banking will remain in effect, but he is in disbelief if any USPS or postal deliveries will be resumed well into the unforeseeable future. This does not answer "What do Project Zebra folks use for cash", Johnson replied. I will arrange for a special reporting session on this within the week and hopefully include explicit options and bank transfers".

To close the mayor's meeting, Andy Moreland from the Bestville Hospital said he had a number of announcements to make about how the hospital was fairing. Briefly, it has all the necessary electricity, air conditioning and supplies. But, they may be running somewhat low in food and certain medications. However, they are in daily touch with distant hospital medical supply warehouses and small air carrier services to pickup and deliver to our airfield runway on some pretext of a weekly "services run." More information to follow

Thanks to the one large Bestville freeze-dry food and supply warehouse on Jefferson Avenue, survival food has about a year's supply on hand, provided there is no large run. They also have some of the more popular medications. All drawdowns of food must be paid for by cash at the time of purchase. No credit extended.

The above is beginning to illustrate the payoff and benefits of Bestville having been chosen as a major experimental EMP template preparation town. So the mayor's office made an assignment to three town folks to provide a near term and longer range recommendations on how it should help support neighboring Towns and Villages. One remarked that the Lord has been good to us and what might we do to help fulfill the Commandment of "Love Thy Neighbor as Thyself". Or, as Kennedy put it, "Ask not what America will do for you, but what together we can do for the freedom of man."

Chapter 5, One Month Later

Bestville, VA (EMP Protected Town), Month 1

At Mayor Henderson's daily "classified meeting" he noticed a decidedly energetic, upbeat and thankful gathering as Bestville was nearly prospering throughout the somewhat otherwise gloom and doom national East Coast, post-EMP situation.

He announced that Virginia Governor Maxwell's office has communicated with the few Virginia EMP protected Towns including Bestville about a proposed flight trip to visit us next week. Three folks would be coming. The mission would be twofold, namely:

(1)- Learn as much as possible about how our own town, Bestville, is faring in the post-EMP event. They want to know all the good, bad and indifferent news, and especially lessons learned. They also wanted a copy of Bestville's daily logs for further study and additives so that others back home and elsewhere in USA can benefit.

(2)- They will conduct a several hour seminar over the local radio conveying how the other EMP protected towns are doing. This will end with an early prediction of what the near-term future appears to offer and when things may get better.

Central and West Coast USA are in good shape as they did not have an EMP burst. But most of the East Coast is in deep trouble. Thanks to the few experimental towns like Bestville, hope is on the rise in some sectors. But the vast majority of other areas have required the National Guard be called to subdue riots and disorders. All the humanitarian services elsewhere are overloaded trying to help out and are now at marginal performance levels.

The National tone is, "If only we became more prepared during 2007-2013 period instead of our apathy, lethargy and other preoccupation, things would have been very different."

The Governor's office air trip to Bestville, also had another hidden mission. Using Bestville as a temporary home, they will set up a small bastion of 25 National Guard on the outskirts of Bestville. The purpose is to distribute water food, medications, clothing and other essentials to desperate regions within about 120 miles of Bestville.

Most of the goods deliveries would be made by restoration vehicles (high payload small trucks). The Guard would also be used to help control the rapid increase of crime outside of Bestville. The Have-Nots are growing, independently, to a non coordinated, small army of serious trouble, robberies, fights, murders and, in some cases, nearing total anarchy.

Mayer Henderson said. "The Governor's office advises that the best way to deal with increasing crime, is to first provide more food and water, and selected medications and a functional clinic (if not a small hospital) capable of X-Raying and Cat Scanning, supported by two resident injury and surgical physicians, two nurses and two ANs. With that in mind, Bestville may receive outside support to convert or construct a hospital with at least 40 beds to help the outlining areas not capable of any clinical support, While potentially controversial to Bestville residents, this has some very compelling arguments".

Mayer Henderson concluded, "I will keep Bestville residents fully informed. In the meantime I will assign two of my office helpers to canvass about 100 Bestville residents to get their views and comments for feedback to the Governor's office.

Finally, banker Rochester reported the following about Project Zebra on retirement pensions, social security, mail and postal deliveries"

"Regarding social security monthly and disability checks, East Coast originating mail services have been handed over to a major hub at Cleveland, OH for government mail only, including monthly Social Security checks. Non-Government mail originating or receiving in the EC EMP region has been "temporarily" suspended. Meanwhile, Fed EX had been contracted to handle this. However, this is available only to EMP protected towns like Bestville, military bases, most Washington, DC government operations, and other undisclosed classified locations.

For private pension plan holders, individual sources have been contacted to use the Fed-Ex Cleveland delivery service. To be sure you have not been left out, use Satellite Phone Service to contact, Fed-Ex, Tempo USPS mail Services, Pension Dept., 1220 Street, Cleveland Ohio, 44101. The big news, however, is that all heretofore mail of EMP protected town pension and SS checks are being changed to be done electronically by bank transfer. Regrettably, and a major goof indeed, is that unprotected towns will receive an unknown distribution with many, if not most, never reaching their intended targets!

Repeating the last sentence for emphasis, retirement moneys from pension funds, retirement sources, annuities, social security, and the like will most likely never reach those towns that have been exposed to an EMP burst. Recipients almost immediately have little to no funds to consider. Some will argue that this is academic as money will rapidly become worthless as things are bought by bartering, anyway. Thank God, that we are Bestville, an EMP protected town.

Chapter 6, Three Months Later

Bestville, VA (EMP Protected Town), Month 3

Mayor Henderson's 7:30 a.m. morning meeting, is now only conducted on the radio station at Bestville where it can reach more listeners than previously at the town square. The time is earlier to enable Bestville employees to hear their office presentation before leaving for work. A repeat broadcast is made at 7:00 p.m. for those missing the morning event.

Police Chief Schultz reported the latest news involves the middle of the night break-in at Well-Mart's Supercenter. This operation is normally closed from midnight to 5:00 a.m. because of the electricity curfew to allow less drain on the solar batteries and generator gas consumption. Apparently, several burglars smashed through the food center entrance driving a narrow truck between the steel guard posts and then crashed through the double sliding doors.. They cleaned the canned fish and canned meat shelves of about $4,500 in goods - all in a few minutes and then exited in their truck right back out the entrance way and into the night, with the store sirens blaring, and emergency outside lighting notwithstanding.

The burglars apparently escaped via a residential region, probably off Howard Street, but none of the four guarded Bestville highway gates reported any activity. So the burglars may still be hidden in some garage within Bestville. All this is very strange since Bestville residents are not suffering from food starvation. Therefore the intruders may be from a location other than Bestville. Remember our orange arm bands. Anyone learning any information, please report to the police at satellite: 434-345-2345 ASAP.

Chief Schultz then turned the discussion back over to the mayor. Mayer Henderson then remarked, "Tuesday is the 3rd month anniversary of the EMP event. Bestville is very fortunate to have about 95% employment since it is estimated from other broadcast receptions that non EMP-protected towns have less than 5% employment and their death rate is very high. Our thanks go to many things which contribute to our advanced EMP protection efforts including our prayers to the Lord.

"One which received little recognition early on, is our 4,000 foot dirt runway landing strip. Last month a C-17 Globemaster III made its first landing. Its single-flight payload limit is 85 tons (170,000 pounds) with conceptually enough food to feed the entire town of Bestville for one week or to replenish our warehouse for about one month. The tanker version of the Globemaster can carry 25,000 gallons of gasoline, enough fuel to permit most vehicles, that are used to get to and from work, to function for nearly one month."

Mayor Henderson then introduced Tony Costello, Town Supervisor.
"I would like to first add to the mayor's remarks that the Governor has authorized Bestville to receive steel mats to place over the dirt air runway, the type used by the military in captured war zones. These mats will reduce accidents from runway potholes due to rain water washout.

"A bastion was set up at Guardpost #1 at Route 360 South town limits for a small 30-unit national guard. Some emergency trucks will be flown in together with a few riot control vehicles and food vans as the state protection and delivery of food and other supplies out to about 120 miles of Bestville. The guard will be setting up a small, EMP-protected solar-PV farm on five acres to provide enough power to handle all their operations."

Costello concluded, "With financial help from Virginia, Bestville has been chosen to set up a second hospital to care for the selected (mostly younger) folks from other neighboring areas where no functional hospitals or clinics exist. Details will be presented tomorrow.

Finally, John. Garwood, Director of our County Economic Development Office, reported the latest findings of their outreach committee, to wit, "As you all know, Bestville was chosen, in a tight competition, as one of a few Towns on the East cost of 18 states from Maine to Florida and west to the Application Mountains. Although we are paying for 85% of our own support, Bestville received some from the state of Virginia and Fed protection. Collectively we represent less than 0.05% (one per 2,000) of the area population."

We have long standing plans to convert the Mills Culture Center into a combination of seminar and education/training center and museum focusing on the entire EMP subject of EMP Protection. This is part of a National plan to make USA citizens more aware of EMP and the many options for EMP protection from small family groups up to large towns of 50,000 people. In one sense, we are following the boy scout memo of "Be Prepared". Truly, this is too late for the recent EMP event, but the Center will be visited by thousands and very active in training in preparation of EMP protection if/when another strikes. More to follow tomorrow."

Garwood said, I have a quick, human-interest story that may be of interest to all. Yesterday afternoon, Carroll Smallvine from Bestville's Northport estates said that every time she touched her new aluminum kitchen window with one hand to open or close the window, and the other hand was on the sink faucet for extended reaching support, she got an electrical shock. A call for help to a neighboring electrician disclosed that a screw to secure the window frame to the wall frame pierced an inside electric cable insulation as well and put 120 volts on the window frame. So when Carroll touched both the window and the faucet at the same time, she got shocked. The fix was simple. Use a shorter, but wider screw which would not reach to the inside wall routed electric circuit wiring.

Chapter 7, One Year Later

Bestville, VA (EMP Protected Town), Year 1

Ironically, Bestville was planning for a one year, EMP anniversary gathering at its new updated Mill River EMP Convention Center and Museum. More than 70 exhibit booths, 4,500 participants and eleven, 1-3 hour EMP seminars lead the main affairs for two days. Most sources are from outside Bestville and the demised East Coast EMP afflicted region.

Little Bestville is being placed on the USA map for EMP activity as the first pilot project to become greatly expanded in the future. The following eleven seminars, projected on a giant 18-foot screen in two halls cover the following subjects:

(1)- An Introduction to EMP - an Historical Overview
(2)- Discussion about EMP vs. Solar Flare Threats
(3)- Contrasting EMP Lifestyles – A Tale of Two Towns
(4)- Lessons Learned from EMP Survivalists
(5)- One EMP Template: A Major Roll for All Economic
       Development Offices.
(6)- How to EMP Shield and Protect Detached Homes, and
       Test Compliance Certifications
(7)- How to Pay for all Costs and Who Pays and ROI
(8)- How to EMP Shield and Protect Commercial and
       Industrial Buildings.
(9)- How to EMP & Solar Flare Protect the local Electric Grid
(10)- How to EMP Protect Town Street and Traffic Lighting
(11)- How to EMP Protect Vehicles and Test Certification

Meanwhile, a major televised program was announced to all active stations in USA. It was being nationally tele- vised, plus webinars and teleconferencing over central and  Western USA. These presentations are extremely important as Nitanyahu of Israel delivered a few HPM (high power microwave) "miniature versions of the EMP" via drone to Iran putting them on notice that Israel will follow with an entire EMP event if Iran does not permit immediate UN inspection of designated facilities within the next two weeks.

Parenthetically, while North Korea has made overtures of sending one or more ICBMs with nuclear warheads headed for western USA, they fully understand that a single retalitory EMP event over North Korea will throw them back into the dark ages of 1870s. However, the fear and watchful alerts remains as a trigger may happen from one or more irrational sources. Thus, the world remains on edge and many speak of the coming of the long promised Armageddon. We shall see......

The End

Hope you enjoyed

Curriculum Vitae of the Author

Don White, registered professional engineer, retd., holds BSEE and MSEE degrees from the University of Maryland. He is past CEO of three Electromagnetic Interference and Compatibility companies in Metro Washington, D.C., one of which traded on the NASDAQ.

Don has written and published 13 technical books over a span of 30 years, which became well known and used worldwide in electronics circles. His last book was "The EMC, Telecom and Computer Encyclopedia Handbook", an 800-page compendium. Don taught over 14,000 engineers via seminars in 39 countries.

At Don White Consultants, he published a bimonthly trade journal called *EMC Technology* magazine circulated over four continents. In addition to being technical editor, he wrote many of the tutorial articles.

Don received the IEEE award for development of automatic spectrum scanning, recording and analysis intercept systems. A 2nd award for contributions to the EMC education and publishing arena. He is a senior member of the former Institute of Radio Engineers and life-time senior member of IEEE. He is past president of IEEE, EMC Society.

Other books by Don White aka Donald R.J. White

- **EMP – Protect Family, Homes and Community, 3rd Edition** REC press, 191 pp. Co-authored with Jerry Emanuelson

- **EMP – Protect Family, Homes and Community, 2nd Edition** REC press, 174 pp.

- **Nuclear EMP Threats – What Next?,** REC Press, 2012, 162 pages

- **Save, Survive and Prosper in an Economy in Crisis**. Dougherty and White, 132 pages, 2008, D-W Press

- **Handbook of Electromagnetic Compatibility,** White and Violette, 2002, Van Nostrand Reinhold

- **The EMF Controversy and Reducing Exposure from Magnetic Fields,** White, Barge, George and Riley, 201 pages, the EEC Press

- **The EMC, Telecom and Computer Encyclopedia, Third Edition,** 800 pages, 1999, *emf-emi control Press*

- **12-Volume Handbook Series,** 1988, The EMC Press:
  - **Vol. 2, Grounding and Bonding,** 487 pages
  - **Vol. 4, Electromagnetic Shielding,** 615, pages
  - **Vol. 6, EMI Test Methodology and Procedures,** 675 pages
  - **Vol. 8, EMI Control Methodology and Procedure,** 544 pages
- **Shielding Design Methodology and Procedures,** 1987, DWCI Press

- **EMI control in the design of printed circuit boards and backplanes,** 1981, DWCI Press

- **A handbook on electromagnetic shielding materials & performance ,** 1975, DWCI Press

- **Five-Volume handbook Series on Electromagnetic Interference and Compatibility,** 1972, DWCI Press

- **Glossary of Acronyms, Abbreviations & Symbols,** 1971, DWCI, Press

- **Methods and Procedures for Automating RFI/EMI Measurement,** 1966, WEI Press

- **Electrical Filters – Synthesis, Design & Applications,** 295 pages, 1966, WEI Press

Appendix A

Ten Tips to Reduce Cost of Electricity up to 60%

Some solar experts say, "For every dollar you put into energy conservation, you can save $3-$5 in the cost of producing your own power."

While going solar is not going to make one wealthy, it is good as an anti-pollutant for the environment, will increase the value of your home, makes us less susceptible to the increasing costs of energy, and not hold USA hostage to foreign oil. As you use our solar calculator, we ask that you think about all the benefits, and not just the bottom line cost and break even. So, it is important in the decision process to identify what you are *trying to optimize* in the first place.

Ten Tips to Reduce Your Electric Bill

First, see remarks on Insulation and "The 3-minute rule," (Part 1). Then, come the 10 tips (Part 2).

Part 1- Insulation

The home insulation status is the largest single factor con-attributing to your electric bill. Fig. 1 shows the five principal areas that must be examined for adequate insulation.

If the house is already built, the options for saving are less. Start by focusing on the

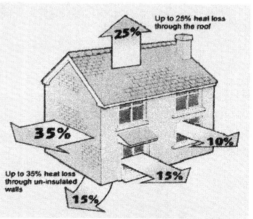

Fig. 1 House showing the five areas of primary heat and cooling loss.

147

heat loss in the attic. Attic fans and extra insulation blown-in or flat fiberglass insulation on the attic floor to attain an R-30± rating is the first step. For basements used in the Northern latitudes in USA, use a 1-2" solid foam between the concrete blocks and the wall-board or knotty pine or other decorative finish to an R-12 rating. Some new insulating paints are available with an R-4 rating.

Leakage at outside door-to frame regions rank second in loss. Change or modify their insulation. Replace any single-pane windows with at least double pane types. Since this latter expense is usually, at least schedule their replacement over a specified time.

Figure 1 also shows other areas which can then be addressed for insulation upgrading.

The Three-Minute Rule

With one exception, this conservation rule requires some discipline and involves no additives. The rule states.

"If you are the only person in a room, watching TV, using electric lights, operating an electric device, and the like, turn off all items if you will be gone for more than three minutes. Exceptions may be a computer under certain conditions (put in a sleep mode instead) or something which may require a reset time or re-operative conditions. If only for a "few minutes", do not turn off and on, as there is some life-expectancy stress in surge, unless a surge suppressor is used in the power line.

The benefits from *the three-minutes rule* may result in your electric bill savings from 8% to 22% (maybe more), if you do nothing else. Thus, in a typical $150/month electric bill, you may save $240±/year.

Part 2 – 10 Tips for Electric Power Conservation

Electrical power is measured in watts and kW; 1 kilowatt = 1,000 watts. Cumulative power over time is measured in units of energy or kW-hours = kiloWatts x hours.

1. Hot-Water Heater (HWH)

The HWH consumes about 10% of your electric load. Reduce its thermostat to about 110° from a typical 125° setting to save wasted money. Search around the house for old blankets and towels to wrap around the heater tank and secure for improved insulation. Or, buy a preformed blanket made specifically for this purpose.

Keep the HWH circuit breaker "off" until 30± minutes before you need hot water for the clothes washer, dishwasher or for personal showering. When you are finished, switch off the breaker.

2. Air Conditioning and Heating Savings

Set the AC to 78° F or somewhat higher in the summer to save electricity. Turn it a bit higher at night or more (say 82°) when away for ½ day or longer. Setting the AC much higher to save more electricity is not advised because of the danger of mold buildup in the Southern coastal states.

When heat pumps are used for winter home heating (even for oil, gas or coal furnaces), set the daytime room temperature to 68°-72°. During the night, upon going to bed, reset the thermostat to 65°. Actually, most new homes in the past 10-15 years have a programmable thermostat. Thus, the different settings can be done to cover a month or a season. Honeywell seems to be the leader in this sector, and they are carried at both Home Depot and Lowes.

3. Washer and Dryer

The Washer–Dryer represents a large electrical load. The

washer costs about $0.04 per load for electricity and about $0.12/load for water. For hot water, the cost is $0.16 + about $0.30 for heated water = roughly $0.40/load. EPA says the average family uses 7.6 loads/wk ($13/month). The big saving is to use fewer loads and at cooler (or cold) water temperature. Have you ever tested to see how well clothes get cleaned using cold water? You may be surprised.

The dryer is the big electrical load. The average drying load consumes roughly about $0.34 in electricity For the average EPA loads of 392/year, the dryer cost $133/year to run. Here, consider some air drying like on wood racks or close lines if no home deed restrictions.

In summary the washer-dryer combination costs about $0.75/load or $295/yr. Cutting down the number of loads, using cold water washing, and drying on racks will save much, if not most, of this cost.

4. Dishwasher

Most of the savings here is not to run the dishwasher unless it is fully loaded with dirty dishes. Small loads, or dishes needed again soon, can be hand washed and placed in a drainage rack to dry. The cost will also be reduced if the hot-water heater was set to 110° F instead of 125° as mentioned above.

5. Pool and Irrigation Pump Motors

Sprinkler or lawn irrigation systems use 1-1.5 horse-power motors and pool pumps also use about 1-1.5 HP motors. A pool heater, when applicable, should use roof solar or butane gas heat) since an electrical heater is very expensive to operate and could double your electric bill (depending on your latitude).

One horsepower in a motor or pump rating corresponds to 746 watts. If you made the mistake of buying a heat pump for your pool, sell it and replace it with a rooftop solar heating or gas heater with the proceeds of the electric heater. You will save big time and use the pool longer as most users quickly learn how expensive it is to electrically-heat a pool.

Many owners will run a pool pump for 4-6 hours in the summer (to combat algae), and 2-3 hours in the winter if in the South (zero in the North as the pool was winterized. If these numbers are reduced to 3 hours in the summer and one in the winter, approximately 60 kWh will be saved in the summer and 45 kWh in the winter. This approximates 630 hours/year, or 950 kWh for a 1.5 HP motor. At an average cost of 13 cents/kWh, the owner in the South will save about $122/year. The Savings in the Northern latitudes is far less.

6. Incandescent Light Bulbs

Traditional incandescent light-bulb filaments are subjected to inrush stress current thereby limiting their life expectancy. Incandescent bulbs from 25 watts to 100 watts can be replaced by the same size fluorescent bulbs which produce comparable light intensity for 25% of the electricity consumption. Fluorescent bulbs also have 10 times longer life expectancy. This is a very compelling reason to replace many if not all incandescent bulbs in the house.

For example, suppose the family room and other areas collectively use eight incandescent bulbs totaling 600 watts for six hours a day. The cost is 600 watts x 6 hrs x $0.13/kW x .001 (kW/watt) = $0.47/day. If you used fluorescent bulbs, the cost savings would be 0.75 x $0.47 = $0.35/day = $10.53/month = $126/year.

The average cost of an incandescent bulb approximates $0.35 and the cost for its fluorescent mate is roughly $1.50 or four times more. However, the life expectancy of the incandescent bulb is less than 1,000 hours, while that of the fluorescent exceeds 5,000 hours. Thus, their replacement costs per lifetimes are somewhat better for fluorescence. Meanwhile the user enjoys one fourth the electricity consumption. (Ed. Note: I have observed about eight fluorescent bulb burn outs in a four period. Thus the life expectancy is questioned).

7. High Duty-Cycle Appliances

Duty cycle means the percentage of the time in use. If the house has two refrigerators, such as one in the garage or for outside patio use, consider disconnecting the outside one as it is expensive to use in the summer (it is also much hotter outside than in the house). Set the kitchen refrigerator to warmer temperatures if it is at or near the coldest setting, which is not needed.

The heating and A/C system duty cycle is also high in the summer and winter, but low in the spring and fall. It was addressed in Subsection 2 above.

8. Low Duty-Cycle Appliances

If the oven and burners are electrical, not much can be done to reduce the electric bill, other than to turn them off when finished using. These are the big kitchen loads, so don't heat up until you are ready to use. The microwave oven shuts off when a selected period for cooking is over. So when the MW can do the lighter cooking, us it in favor of the oven and burners. Remember, don't turn on the MW oven with no load placed therein as damage may result or keystroke life shortened.

Turn off the coffee maker after use or put it on a timer. Some people let it run for hours; then, turn it off.

A ceiling fan takes about 100 watts or about 2-5% of an A/C load. Run one or more it at low speed, if needed. This can reduce some of the A/C duty cycle. This also keeps hot food from cooling on the counters.

9. Den and Office

Most computers today are laptops (15-45 watts; desk-tops consume 60-250 watts) and consume about four times the power of a desktop computer. The LCD screen in a laptop consumes most of the power, typically about 30 watts.

Many laptop computer owners add a 19-23 inch LCD external screen as it is easier to read than smaller print. The power consumption is correspondingly more (roughly 50 watts). Modern computers have internal "sleep" modes when not in use for a while (they power down to 3-5 watts), which time is internally settable. Thus, when leaving a computer for a half hour or longer, place it in the sleep mode. Turn it off during the night when not in use.

Supporting printers, copiers, scanners and the like should be turned off when not in use. Some standby modes waste power.

10. Outside Lighting

Nearly all outdoor lighting should be put on timers which cost less than $10 each. With the new fluorescent light bulbs, where appropriate (flame shaped decorative incandescent bulbs do not yet have a fluorescent counterpart), the cost to operate outside lighting be-comes 25% of the older incandescent bulbs.

Finally, solar outdoor lights tend to become a waste of money as the batteries have to be replaced each year at $2 apiece or $4 per lamp. Low-voltage AC lighting is more cost effective since the bulbs last much longer than the battery life of solar outdoor lighting.

The Bottom Line:

Of course, if you are already doing many of the above electricity-saving conservation steps, your options to save will be considerably less. Otherwise, when all the dollar savings above are added up for the typical $150/month electric bill, they approximate $65-$80/month or $850±/year. This is equal to 47±% savings. Note: this is also roughly equal to about what you would save if you invested in a solar rooftop electric system saving equal to 50% of your electric bill. And, except for the insulation cost mentioned above, it costs you nothing except, possibly, a change in yourself discipline attitude about conservation.

EMP-Protect Family, Homes and Community

by Don White, PE, MSEE

EMP Solutions. Renewable Energy Creations, LLC

Jerry Emanuelson, BSEE

Futurescience, LLC

An innovative approach to EMP (electromagnetic pulse) protection that can allow entire communities to maintain their "pre-pulse" lifestyle.

Many things could cause the long term loss of the electric power grid upon which we all depend, including geomagnetic storms and cyberterrorism.

High-altitude EMP is a unique form of destruction, however, that adds the loss of most of our vital electronic infrastructure to the electric power grid devastation. The electronic infrastructure includes telecommunications of all kinds, inventory control, personal computers and most forms of modern transportation.

In this book, you will learn how to use electromagnetically shielded solar photovoltaic panels to provide electricity through all kinds of electric power grid outages, whether the outage lasts for hours or for years.

You will also learn relatively inexpensive means for electromagnetically shielding volumes from the size of a pantry to a large building in order to protect the items inside from EMP. New methods of financing EMP protection for communities -- from homeowners associations to county governments -- are also addressed. Available at www.emp-safeguard.com/new-2.html, $19 postpaid

Made in the USA
Charleston, SC
23 June 2015